MARLOW

ANDY BRIGGS

TANGLEBOX

BOOKS

MARLOW
nightmares can come true

MARLOW

Copyright © 2020 by Andy Briggs

Cover art: Shutterstock

www.andybriggsbooks.com
Twitter: @abriggswriter
Instagram: @itsandybriggs

MARLOW

---

sign up for Andy's
NEWSLETTER

info@andybriggsbooks.com

or say hello on Twitter:

@abriggswriter

MARLOW

Cover art: Shutterstock

www.andybriggsbooks.com
Twitter: @abriggswriter
Instagram: @itsandybriggs

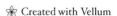 Created with Vellum

CHAPTER ONE

THE RAPPING at the door was loud and persistent. A middle-aged pretty woman answered it with equal urgency. Her black hair was pulled so tight into a smart ponytail that the skin was taut against her clearly defined cheekbones. For several seconds she stared in surprise at the malodorous tramp on the doorstep. And several more to register it was a woman.

"Bryony Glass?" the tramp asked as she gruffly cleared her throat.

"Y-yes."

"You called my. About your son."

The tramp raised an unkempt eyebrow expectantly. Bryony's father, Boris, joined her at the door, carefully angling it so that the stranger couldn't see into their well-appointed home. Boris's brow furrowed and his nostrils automatically twitched at the sour aroma standing on the doormat.

"Can I help you?" Boris Glass demanded with as much authority as his five-foot-six frame could deliver. He pushed his glasses firmly up his nose and looked as if he wished he had something to block the stench out.

The tramp ran a hand through her lank hair, then risked a casual sniff under her left armpit. Even with the thick trench coat she could detect something unpleasant, although she conceded that could have been the coat itself.

"Marlow Cornelius. You called me." When the Glasses looked at her blankly she felt compelled to add: "About the kid?"

Comprehension flooded their faces and a little gasp of "Ooohh!" escaped their lips in unison.

"Sorry, of course," puffed Bryony as it suddenly dawned on her how rude she had been. "I just didn't expect you to... um..."

"Be a woman?"

"Be so early," Boris quickly chimed in. He looked expectantly around the doorstep. "Did you bring anything? Any *specialist* equipment?"

Marlow opened her long coat revealing a modified sawn-off shotgun, the barrel of which flared outward like a hunting blunderbuss. She patted the scarred walnut stained hilt.

"Right here."

Bryony smiled. "Jolly good," she said weakly. After all, it was what they were paying for and services like Marlow's were far from cheap. She opened the door wide. "Dan is upstairs, asleep."

Marlow wiped her runny nose with the hem of her filthy jacket, then pumped the blunderbuss with a loud CLICK-CLACK that echoed through the still night air. She entered the house and the heavy oak front door slammed shut behind her.

DAN GLASS WAS FAST ASLEEP.

For a thirteen-year-old kid like Dan that was no surprise. He suffered from narcolepsy, a condition that sent him headlong asleep at the most inopportune moments. He had lost count of the number of times he'd started snoring midway through giving an answer in class. MRIs showed nothing. Pills only had a limited effect, as did caffeine. In short, it was a debilitating condition Dan and his parents could do nothing about. Now the condition had started to attract even bigger and more unusual problems.

Marlow Cornelius gently pushed open the bedroom door and crept inside. She could have entered with rock music pumping and Dan still wouldn't have stirred. Out of habit, Marlow gently closed the door behind her and slid the chair from Dan's desk, positioning it at the end of the bed. There she sat with the blunderbuss across her lap and waited.

Patience was not a virtue Marlow was born with, yet it was a vital one her profession demanded. *Profession*... there was an unjust phrase. Marlow was born into the family business and her father had drilled into her the importance of carrying it on, right up until he had...

Marlow forced the grim memories from her mind and concentrated on Dan. The boy's eyes were rapidly moving under closed eyelids. He was deep in REM sleep, caught up in a dream. Marlow felt a pang of jealousy. She never dreamed. Unlike those annoying people in the bar who claimed they didn't dream either, when in fact just didn't remember them, Marlow *really* didn't dream. Ever. She had never experienced the joy of stepping into another reality; the pleasure of meeting incredible characters who existed only in her mind's eye; or enjoyed the thrill of being a heroic warrior.

She'd never had a dream to follow.

She hated people who did. Loathed them. Staring at Dan lost in another world made Marlow seethe with envy. She dragged her gaze away from the boy and studied the pile of books at the side of the bed, most of them unread as Dan couldn't make it past the first chapter before his eyes clamped shut. The bedside table light was decorated with figures from anime movies. Marlow didn't know which; she never got the chance to go anywhere.

Then she noticed that the lamp's ceramic body had been glued back together from a fall. Paying more attention, she saw that the wallpaper behind was torn - three diagonal slashes that looked as if powerful talons had swiped down. The angle suggested that they came from the direction of the bed, but each mark was as least two of the boy's fingers in width. Now she was looking for it, the room bore many signs of previous struggles. The carpet was torn in places, furniture scuffed as if something large had passed by, and the back of the door - that sent shivers down Marlow's spine - savage claws had torn chunks of wood from it. She noted that the door wasn't a normal bedroom one but a heavy wooden fixture, more like a front door. Designed to keep somebody out.

Or something in.

Dan mumbled incoherently in his sleep. Marlow regretted shutting the door and turned back to Dan just in time to see the table lamp dim. The bulb wasn't faulty; it burned with the same brightness - but the surrounding shadows grew denser, soaking up the illumination like a sponge.

Marlow's fingers tightened around the shotgun, but she didn't move. She focused on keeping her breathing steady. Panic was not a friend in these circumstances. She'd done this routine many times before, yet somehow, for some intangible reason, this felt different.

Dan grumbled in his slumber, unaware of what was happening in the waking world. The illumination had now dropped to near twilight levels, velvet shadows were cast in all the usual trouble spots: under the bed and across the closet door.

Marlow's ears pricked when she heard the noise: a low chittering that sounded like a distant locust swarm ready to descend. It came from the darkness and rose in volume, slowly evolving into a growl that came from beneath the bed. The throaty bass was so deep that Marlow felt her ribs vibrate. She angled sideways on the chair so she could get a better look under the bed, but Dan's hanging duvet blocked the view.

Marlow berated herself for doing this sober. She had a vague sense of pride for not drinking for several weeks now, but that accomplishment was swiftly becoming a problem. Drink might be damaging her health but at least it helped keep terror at bay. A cold chill pricked the back of her neck and her breath became visible in short smoky puffs as the temperature plummeted. She slipped from the chair and knelt down, using the gun barrel to lift the duvet aside, tensing in anticipation of an attack.

There was nothing under the bed. Except a pair of crusty socks that had fermenting for so long that their odour overpowered Marlow's own stale musk.

Then she sensed movement behind. Marlow's shoulders sagged as she realised her mistake. Nightmares - you could never trust them. And you should never turn your back on them.

In the reflection of a small sticker-covered mirror that hung on the wall, Marlow could see the black mass of darkness coil into a solid shape. It looked panther-shaped, with matte black skin instead of fur, and an oversized mouth with hundreds of needle-like teeth in a slavering maw. Luminous blue eyes burned with an inhuman malevolence.

It was a sight that could, and indeed literally did, freeze the blood.

But not Marlow's; her blood was too thick. She had been studying the nightmares for as long as she could remember and knew the beast's linage, even if its hunting methods were irregular.

Feline quadru-nightmaris, she mentally rattled off before the creature rose on its four hind legs, revealing an extra pair of thin forward legs that ended in a lethal pair of serrated hooks designed to pull victims closer to the gnashing teeth. *Feline sextulus-nightmaris* she corrected herself. *Crap.*

This was not just an irregularity – this was something new. And if there was one thing in the world Marlow didn't like, it was *new*.

She swung the gun under her arm so it was upside down, but at least facing the general direction of the foe. Her finger snapped backwards and pulled the trigger.

BRYONY JUMPED when she heard the gunshot upstairs. It was followed by an almighty crash that didn't seem to want to end. The ceiling light swung frantically and she was convinced the roof would cave in. Even as she watched, cracks formed across the plaster and hanging Christmas decorations trembled. Boris refused to meet his daughter's gaze. He just stared at the television and hitched the volume up so the audience laughter masked the destruction in Dan's room.

More splintering wood followed another ear-splitting gunshot. Bryony made a mental note that they would need to purchase another desk for Dan. She'd never liked that one anyway.

MARLOW SLID out a desk drawer and swung it across the beast's head. It broke on contact but did nothing to faze the creature which was flat on its back, rolling amongst the desk's debris. Dan was still fast asleep, smiling, oblivious to the racket from the battle.

A clawed foot struck Marlow in the stomach, knocking the breath from her. She staggered backwards across the room; a flailing hand tore a poster off the wall as she slammed against the window. She heard, and felt, a pane of glass crack under her shoulder blade.

The nightmare thrashed on its back, trying to roll upright but hampered by its own scything fore-claws. Two plate-sized gunshot wounds to the chest had only slowed it a little. The pale blue wounds had pumped thick blue blood before the wound had frozen with icy crystals that automatically stemmed the bleeding. This was a tough opponent, and Marlow was badly out of shape, used to hunting down smaller Infiltrators. Her fingers scrambled for a pair of fresh shotgun cartridges held in loops on her belt.

The beast finally flipped onto its four rear legs - just as Marlow breached the barrel open across her arm. The monster furiously shook itself clear of the splinters like a dog.

Marlow slid the first cartridge into the barrel of the specially designed duel-barrel blunderbuss. A weapon originally favoured by Victorian elephant hunters and refined by Nightmare Hunters. Cobalt lupine eyes locked onto her and the nightmare howled as it sprung forward.

A second cartridge was loaded as the creature arced through the air. Marlow allowed herself to slide down the window - landing hard on her ass. She felt the pain of sitting on something sharp, an errant plug probably. With a flick of the wrist, she locked the barrel back into place and pulled the trigger—

The nightmare was destined for the window the moment Marlow dropped. The twin gunshots blew its ugly head into indigo icy particles that splattered and stained the walls. Its was slain before it crashed through the glass, dragging the curtains with it. The corpse vaporised before impacting the floor, leaving just a mess of broken glass, a splintered window frame and some unsightly paisley curtains.

Marlow let the gun fall to her side and expelled a long sigh. The eradication had been a lot tougher than she'd anticipated. Her mouth was dry and craving alcohol – preferably Southern Comfort. It would also numb the aches that pulsed across her body.

Dan rolled over in his sleep and let out a contented grunt.

MARLOW WAITED IMPATIENTLY on the doorstep as Dan's mum wrote out a cheque. She glanced at the pool of broken glass on the grass outside. Dan's room and wondered why the Infiltrator had acted so out of character. In all her experience, they stuck to the same routine. They were not creatures blessed with vivid imaginations...

Her musing was cut short as Bryony shoved the cheque in her hand and mumbled "goodnight". Marlow checked it was for the right amount and just turned back in time to see the door close in her face.

With a sigh, she slid the fee in her pocket and trudged back to her dilapidated Beetle car. Her mouth may be demanding a drink, but her brain needed sleep. Unfortunately, as usual, it would be a dreamless sleep.

CHAPTER TWO

DAN GLASS YAWNED and his eyelids fluttered uncontrollably. Before he knew it, his head lolled and sharply knocked against the car window. The jolt made him sit bolt upright and he forced himself to look out of the car window, focusing on anything to keep him awake. It was an exercise his doctor had recommended, but Dan found it difficult.

Bench. Bus. Girls walking to school. Pigeon. Man with an obvious wig.

"Feeling alright?" said his Grandpa from the driver's seat. He angled the rear-view mirror to get a better look at Dan.

"Sure. Great." Dan's mind felt fluffy as narcolepsy fogged his brain, ready to pounce.

"How did you sleep? I mean, do you remember your, um, dreams?"

Dan shook his head. His dreams were sometimes vague shadow memories of things he had experienced. Other times they were vivid and vibrate; fun and surreal. But lately, they had become... scary. He didn't want to alarm his mother. It didn't look like she was getting any sleep either, and he didn't

want her to worry any more about him. She had been doing
that for far too long.

Boris reached for a capped thermos cup wedged in the car's
drinks holder and handed it to Dan.

"Coffee, just the way you like it."

Dan took the cup, opened the cap, and took a mouthful of
the sweet hot liquid. He knew he shouldn't really be drinking
coffee at his age, but he found it was one of the few things that
kept him awake even if the caffeine was losing its edge. At least
it was better than the army of prescriptions he had been given
over the years. None of them ever worked and he had increasingly become suspicious the doctors were using him for
nothing more than a training ground.

"Thanks."

Boris didn't bother asking any more questions on the drive
to school, and Dan managed to stay awake and alert for the
rest of the journey. He felt comfortable with his Grandpa who
understood his condition almost as well as the doctors, and
nothing else needed to be said. Dan exited outside school and
stared at the soulless grey building; his prison for the next six
hours.

He made it through the school yard gauntlet, never stopping to speak or say hello. What was the point? His two best
friends had left - one when his parents relocated for work and
the other... Dan wasn't so sure what the reasons were exactly,
but his friend had stopped talking to him after a sleepover and
then the family left the country shortly afterwards.

The sanctuary of the school library lay just ahead. Just a
few more yards to the tranquil refuge...

"Alright, Hypnos," growled a voice from his left.

Dan sagged as Barry Maven hove into view and blocked his
path. He was a foot taller than Dan and considerably wider as
most of him was muscle. He was the school's top soccer player

and currently ranked as the number one bully. Jenkins and Pith were his two cackling henchmen. What they lacked in physical presence they made up for in ugly. They were the perfect wingmen to Maven's chiselled leading-man looks and groomed black hair that caught the attention of every girl in school. What was worse than having a bully whom all the girls fancied? Well, having one who was also smart didn't help one bit.

"Hypnos?" said Dan. "What, so I'm going to hypnotise you now? Make you punch yourself in the face?"

"Hypnos, Greek god of sleep, doofus." Maven shoved Dan so hard in the shoulder that he almost fell to the floor. "And don't try and get smart with me or I'll shove your molars down your trachea."

Dan blinked, trying to work out what the threat actually was. That was the problem with Maven, he baffled you with his banter then punched you in the face when you were trying to figure it out. Dan gripped the strap of his backpack. He was carrying some heavy book, which would make a handy weapon, and he wasn't beyond retaliation. He'd done it before, not that it did him any good. In fact, it landed Dan in a whole world of pain and no amount of complaining to the teachers would get them to believe Maven, their role model pupil, was a thug.

"Well, you got me," said Dan. "You've just punched my brain into the land of confusion."

"You got a phone?"

Dan felt more comfortable with comprehensible threats. "Like the one you stole off me last month? I should have got you arrested for that only I had no phone to call the police–"

Maven snarled, flashing his perfect teeth. He gripped Dan's arm so hard that it tingled as the circulation cut off. "You're no hero, squirt. Condescending verbalization's not going to gain you any approbation. Got that?"

"No!" squealed Dan convinced his arm was turning blue. "It's like being beaten up by a thesaurus! What the hell are you talking about?" He felt somebody rummage in his backpack, and Pith pulled the thermo cup out.

"What's this?"

"A cup, you moron!" snapped Dan. He was rapidly losing his patience, and being bullied by somebody called *Pith* was an injustice in itself. Maven slapped Dan around the ear. It wasn't a hard blow, but it sent his ears ringing and his balance disappeared as the floor turned to jelly.

Pith flipped the cup's lid open and inhaled deeply - then gagged on the pungent smell within.

"Coffee? Urgh! I hate coffee, you little freak!" Pith threw the cup down.

"NO!" Dan tried to reach for it, but it was too late. The plastic cracked on the flagstones and brown liquid spread across the concrete.

"Bet you needed that to stay awake, didn't ya, freak?" grinning Pith, delighted with a deduction worthy of Sherlock Holmes.

Maven released his power grip on Dan's now numb arm. "Laters, Morph."

Dan stared at the coffee draining down the cracks between the flagstones. "Morph?" he said, more to himself.

Maven and his thugs were already several yards away, but he still heard and spun around. "Morpheus - God of dreams, dingus! Don't you learn anything in this place?"

The bell rang, summoning children to education. Dan rubbed the life back into his arm and turned away from the library. Without the caffeine perking him up the day was going to go a whole lot quicker.

. . .

"BUT OF COURSE, it was forced on King John by feudal barons eager to protect their own interests..." droned a voice so monotonous that Dan had already forgotten his history teacher's name. "The most important change was... Mr Glass?"

Dan nodded dreamily. Yes, *he* was the most important change.

His eyelids dropped.

The teacher's hand slammed on the desk so hard Dan jumped - his eyes flicked open to see the man's hideous old face inches from his own.

"We will not be falling asleep in my lesson, will we, Mr Glass?"

Dan's cheeks burned the moment he realised that he'd been nodding off. He heard giggling next to him. A group of girls were finding his embarrassment funny; amongst them Jade Harrow. She flicked her long blonde hair from her face to reveal that dazzling smile... a smile that was aimed squarely at Dan's discomfort. He came crashing back to earth as the teacher's stale breath hit him.

"The *Magna Carta* is one of the most important events in history! Why is that?"

Dan tried to recall something. Anything. But his mind had confused reality with the swirling ramblings of his near-slumbering subconscious.

"Because... um..."

The teacher backed off, scowling critically at Dan. "I don't know why I bother. Anyone else know the answer?"

Dan slid down in his chair as a sea of hands shot up around him. At least the embarrassment would keep him conscious until the end of the lesson. He glanced at Jade, but she was looking firmly at the whiteboard, oblivious to his existence.

Lunchtime came and went, and Dan was pleased that he could stay awake. He had found some loose change in his various pockets and slipped out of school to the nearby newsagents so he could buy an energy drink to replace the coffee. He didn't like the taste but felt the immediate effects of the *taurine* it contained. Dan had once Googled the ingredients of everything he ate and drank to see if there was anything there that could account for his narcolepsy. Taurine was commonly found in bile – and the drink tasted like it too, but it worked as advertised.

He walked back to school with a spring in his step - narrowly avoiding Maven and his lackeys as he sneaked through the yards to spend the rest of his lunch in the solitude of the library.

The bell rang, marking the start of Dan's next lesson. The one he dreaded the most: maths. Not that he disliked maths, he didn't, but it was the one class he shared with Maven. Jade was there too, always giving Maven wide-eyed looks and flashed her dazzling smile at everything he said.

Dan sat in the corner and tried to shield his face with a textbook. The lesson was only five minutes in when a pen thumped into his book, followed by another. He tried to ignore the sniggering Maven and concentrated on the gibberish on the page. Trigonometry, what use was that in the real world?

Through the window he saw storm clouds gathering in the sky and swore he saw a flicker of lightning. He always felt nervous during storms. As a child, his grandmother had always sat with him in a dark cupboard during storms so they couldn't see the lightning. She was convinced it would seek them out, strike them, and transport them to God knows where.

As he stared at the pages the equations danced around the paper, making them impossible to fathom. Heavy rain began hammering the window at the same time Maven hurled a heavy textbook at Dan's head. Dan looked up in time to see the book before the corner cracked him on the forehead. His chair legs snapped and he toppled backwards, crashing to the floor.

He could feel blood from the gash on his forehead trickle down his face and his exploratory fingers confirmed he was bleeding. Maven laughed, pointing a finger at him. To make matters worse, so was everybody else, including the teacher.

Dan's face contorted into a scowl and his fingers curled into fists - and at that moment the windows imploded into the classroom, showering glass over everybody, as a giant gorilla leapt through. It punched Maven to the floor, beat on his chest a few times and then began chasing the mocking pupils as they fled, screaming, towards the door.

Dan closed his eyes. It was funny. The terror on their faces was worth it. Their terrified yelling sounded far off, as if on the edges of a dream. He shifted his arms to get more comfortable. The crashing noises increased, as did the wails of anguish around him, but the cacophony blended into soothing sounds of torment. He was sure he'd heard his name being called, but it was distant and growing fainter. Besides, who would be calling his name?

THE NUMBER of ambulances that had turned up had surprised Dan. Almost everybody in the class had been injured when the window shattered. Firefighters were already erecting scaffolding as some incredible force, presumably from a lightning strike, had smashed parts of the supporting wall aside. The heavy rain wasn't helping anybody, especially as it was now turning to snow.

Worried parents had arrived shortly after the police vans, which discharged officers who instantly began searching the grounds. Boris squeezed his Grandson's shoulder and angled the umbrella to cover them both a little better.

"Are you sure you are not hurt?"

"I'm fine."

"And you didn't see anything?" Dan noticed the tension in his Grandpa's voice.

"I must have fallen asleep," said Dan. "Typical, isn't it? The only day an escaped gorilla trashes the school and I slept through it! What were the odds?"

At least that's what the confused pupils thought they had seen. Nobody could give a clear description as the storm clouds had blocked the sun, turning day into night, and the room's lights sparked and failed. They recounted how the fast moving beast had smashed desks and overturned bookcases before it bit a chunk from the teacher's leg, broke various ribs, arms and legs of three students - including Maven - before smashing through the wall as it fled.

Boris squeezed his Grandson's shoulder harder, but didn't comment.

"Do you think they'll find it?"

"I'm sure it's long gone," said Boris firmly.

"I wanted to thank it for beating up Maven," said Dan, almost to himself. He had watched Maven being loaded onto the ambulance and heard he'd suffered several broken bones. Curiously, Dan felt an absolute absence of guilt.

"We should get you home." Dan wasn't going to argue with that. "And I think it best you spend the rest of the week out of school too."

Dan wasn't going to argue with that either.

AN ANSWER MACHINE would be the solution to all her problems. Or at least the one she currently had. Marlow jammed the pillow over her ears and rolled over in bed. Unfortunately the threadbare pillow had little stuffing left and the ringing telephone showed no signs of abating.

With a grunt of effort, Marlow rolled from her crumpled bed, still fully clothed, a usual precaution as her spacious studio apartment was freezing. In a former life, it had been a sought after glamourous space, but a couple of years of neglect, and the lack of cash - and interest - had taken its toll. Marlow winced when she stepped on a cold half-eaten kebab on the floor. She felt the thick sauce ooze through the gaps in her socks. Tracing the landline cable snaking across the floor, she kicked aside three empty wine bottles and found the yellowing plastic phone under a horde of home delivery menus she had gathered over the years. She cleared her throat with one long disgusting hawk, spat on the floor, then picked up the phone.

"Marlow Cornelius."

An angry raised voice shouted from the other end of the line.

"What? Whoa, whoa calm down. What?"

The one-sided rant continued with just a few grunts of acknowledgement from Marlow as she searched the apartment for her logbook. She eventually found it under a stack of newspapers and opened the thick ledger. It comprised of yellowing pages that progressively became newer as they reached the back. She found the most recent entries and ran a dirty finger down the column of names. She tapped the last name as the abuse from the phone continued. The job was only from the previous night, so she shouldn't need reminding, but her inability to dream was seriously affecting her memory. Dan Glass. It all came back to her.

"Understood," she said, stopping the caller in mid-rant. "Your case was a little odd but - no I don't - but... this is a family business handed through the generations..." She wiped her nose on her sleeves. Family business... didn't she just know it was. A business she had been forced into...

Then a word cut through her inner monologue, a word she'd never heard before. One that sent a chill down her spine.

"*Refund*? No, no... look. I don't do that. No... well, it hasn't ever happened before. Look calm down. I'll be right around and see what we can sort out."

She slammed the phone down before Mr Glass could refuse. Never in her life, in the business's history, had a Cornelius been asked for a refund. She better quickly nip this problem in the bud.

CHAPTER THREE

MARLOW WINCED when she sipped the coffee, which Bryony Glass had made at some unsafe industrial strength. Her taste buds had immediately shut down, and she was surprised the drink hadn't melted the cup. She shuddered involuntarily and glowered at Dan from across the kitchen table. The boy drank with no obvious signs of being about to spasm uncontrollably from the caffeine intake.

"So, let's get this straight. It happened during the day?"

Dan shrugged. "I fall asleep all the time."

His Mum and Grandpa swapped nervous glances.

"But the *day*?" Marlow couldn't hide her incredulous tone.

"There have never been any... *incidents* during the day before," said Bryony, giving a meaningful look towards Dan.

Marlow knew that look. She had seen it on hundreds of parents. It was the look that said the adults hadn't informed their children what *really* happens when they fall asleep. Bastards. Marlow rubbed her eyes, why was she always the idiot who had to enlighten them?

Dan laughed. "Incidents? You mean like a gorilla barging

into school? That must have been amazing." His face scrunched in annoyance. "And I slept through it all," he added with contempt.

"And you did say your services were, um... *guaranteed*," said Boris Glass quietly.

Dan frowned. He might live in a perpetual cloud of tiredness, but he was not dumb. Marlow felt the boy's eyes bore into her.

"Who are you? You from the animal rescue? The zoo?"

"Sort of," said Marlow, leaning back in the chair and glancing out of the window. A few Christmas decorations couldn't disguise the fact that the winter nights were rapidly pulling in, and the snow had continued throughout the day. It was almost the perfect weather for Them. "What do you recall?"

Dan shrugged. "Bits. I didn't even know I was asleep. I dreamt of being in the lesson and... and kids were messing about." Dan looked into his cup and Marlow could see that he was editing his recollection, whether consciously or not. "Then the windows smashed into the class. You know how sometimes your dreams are affected by the real world? Like an alarm clock goes off, but in your dream it's a burglar alarm or something?"

That was outside Marlow's field of life experience, so she remained silent but nodded politely.

Dan slurped his coffee. Apparently the detailed analysis of his dream was over.

"Has anyone told you what happens when you go to sleep?"

Marlow noticed both adults go rigid and slightly pale. She didn't care, the boy needed to know the truth and the threat of having to issue a refund meant she needed to go the extra mile.

"The doctors told me all about my narcolepsy. It's a neurological sleep disorder, which means I'm always tired in the day and can fall asleep instantly. I get cataplexy, which means my muscles go weak so I could even collapse asleep while standing in a queue. Which happens a lot." Dan reeled off the facts as if they were a normal problem rather than a life debilitating disorder. "It takes most people ninety minutes to enter REM sleep, that's when you dream. With narcoleptics it takes ten minutes. It takes me twenty seconds," he added with a trace of pride.

Marlow was surprised by the kid's straightforward attitude towards his condition. She had always made life a misery for anybody who was willing to listen to her own problems which, even she had to begrudgingly admit, were not as awful as Dan's.

"That's... right," said Marlow, trying to word her next phrase carefully. "But what I meant was, what happens when *you* go asleep."

"I don't know what you mean."

Marlow hawked in her throat, before realizing she was in company. She swallowed it with a long sip on her coffee, then broke into a hacking choke for several seconds as the bitter taste pummelled the back of her throat. After Bryony gave her a glass of water and her eyes had stopped streaming, she continued, aware that the kid was regarding her as some kind of clown.

"When normal people, er, I mean most people have dreams they're nothing more than figments of their imaginations." She always found it difficult to describe dreams. It's always difficult to talk about something you have never experienced before. "Even nightmares. They can be caused by all kinds of things: stress, watching a horror movie, some foods even mess your mind. Some people dream very vividly when they have nightmares, so vivid they think they're real. They call them night terrors. They're extremely scary, so severe that folks wake up screaming in cold sweats."

"That has never happened to me."

"No, that's because you don't find night terrors as scary as everybody else. Yours sort of numb you to the terror they give off so you don't wake up. You see, you're a *special* kind of kid. You're a Conduit."

"I've been called a lot of things before," said Dan carefully, "but what's a Conduit?"

"It's a channel. Y'see, when you sleep you open up a portal between the nightmares, which are very real creatures that exist in their own dimension, and our world. They can come through."

Dan's eyes went wide. "Come through? You mean, monsters can just walk out of my head and into this kitchen?"

"Yup."

Dan's look of astonishment lasted for a whole ten seconds - before he barked with laughter and thumped the table with the palm of his hand so hard that the cups almost toppled over. "Ha, ha! That's funny! You're so funny!"

He continued chuckling, but his mirth gradually faded when he realized the adults were not joining in. Their stony concern had no place for humour.

"Come on! You've got to be kidding!" said Dan. "What am I? Four? You can't just tell me there's a monster under my bed and expect me to believe it!" He glanced at his Mum and Grandpa and was alarmed to see they were nodding.

"You've seen the broken furniture in your room," said Boris.

"You said I was sleepwalking!"

"And the claw marks on the wall," Bryony added.

"That was me acting out my dreams! You told me..." The hysteria in Dan's voice was rising.

"They lied," said Marlow calmly but firmly. She saw the adults bristle with indignation - but they had the decency to look guiltily away. "When you have nightmares, they are real creatures from someplace else, trying to push through into our world. They want to be here and your sort gives them the chance."

Dan tried to speak, but the enormity of what he was being told stole his words. Plus, he disliked the term *your sort*.

"When you sleep, you're the only one safe because they need you. Last night I was sitting at the end of your bed when a particularly nasty critter came through and tried to bite my head off. I shot it and threw it outta the window."

Dan gasped. He had obviously noticed the broken window the instant he woke up that morning. "B-but Grandpa said a bird flew through it."

Marlow shot Boris an incredulous look. "A bird? That's all you could think of? Was it a pterodactyl?"

"I had to make something up on the spot!" Boris snapped back.

Dan looked at his Grandpa with wide eyes. "Is this true?"

Marlow answered for him. "You hear of people seeing weird things in the night, monsters in the closet, strange big cats prowling country lanes, UFOs, they're all Infiltrators from the other side. A nightmare realm built in what we call Inner-space; the place where dreams live, or at least the creatures that lurk in them. My family has been fighting them for generations."

"Why?"

Marlow shrugged. "Somebody has to, right? And we have certain... skills needed to do it."

"Miss Cornelius *supposedly* banished your nightmare last night," said Bryony, squeezing Dan's hand.

"So what happened in school... that wasn't an escaped gorilla?"

"You really think that could've happened? A gorilla? Your

classmates probably thought that's what it was because it vaguely resembled one, but it would have been too confusing for them to make out anything specific. At least, any of the horrific details."

Dan looked thoughtful. "So, if you banished my nightmare... why did I have one again today?"

"That's exactly what we would like to know," said Boris, folding his arms and leaning back in his chair. "What happened to your guarantee? You're not one of these rogue traders are you?"

"It's not my fault your kid's a freak!" snapped Marlow more harshly than she would have liked. She noticed Dan cringe at the insult, but her professional reputation was at stake here - even if she didn't want such a reputation. "I got rid of the nightmare. What he manifested today was a *daymare,* and that is a completely different price sheet."

"So I had both?" asked Dan. There was fear in his voice now as he slowly grasped the reality he was being fed.

"Obviously," Marlow huffed. "But you shouldn't be able to do that."

"Why not?"

"Conduits are fragile things. I don't mean you physically, I mean up here." She tapped his head. "The Infiltrators have to work long and hard to get through. It can take months. Once that beastie comes into our world and I kill it - it's *dead.* Therefore, their Conduit should close right up. But you..."

"I'm a freak."

Marlow hesitated. She was about to agree, but some part of her knew that wasn't the socially acceptable thing to do right now. She changed tact.

"Daymares are rare. Very rare. Sure, people who work night shifts can form a Conduit, but the Infiltrators really don't like daylight very much. It must have been desperate to get through for some reason."

"That still doesn't explain how he had two of those - those things," said Bryony.

"I thought that whole–" Marlow mouthed the word 'freak', "–thing explained that?"

Dan scowled at her. "So will it happen again, *Miss Expert?*"

Marlow had disliked this kid the moment a refund was mentioned, but now she hated him. She drummed her fingers on the table as she tried to recall any reports of such a thing happening.

"This is unprecedented. If you want my professional opinion, 'cause that's what you're paying for, then I suspect the answer is going to be: yeah."

Bryony gasped and Boris rubbed the bags under his eyes. It was obvious that they were both at breaking point.

In almost a whisper, Boris spoke up. "Then what can we do?"

Marlow smiled. "Well, first of all, I think we need to discuss my *rates*."

DAN REFUSED TO SLEEP.

"Come on, kid. I thought you were a narcoleptic? Out like a light?"

"Usually. But there's something that's keeping me awake. It's working better than caffeine."

"What?"

"Well... I don't know if it's the big smelly troll in my bedroom or the shotgun resting across her knees."

"Blunderbuss," Marlow corrected as she scowled at him. If it were not for the dreaded refund then she would have been happy to walk away from the pain in the ass and let him suffer his nightmares.

Maybe that wasn't completely true. Nobody should have to suffer Infiltration - that's the term her Grandpa coined when compiling the *Book of Nightmares* for all future hunters. It was actually more of a scrapbook filled with spelling mistakes, until he'd added intricate details and impressively bound it for no other reason other than making it difficult to misplace.

"And I don't smell that bad," Marlow added.

"Trust me, you really do. Don't you have a family? A husband? Somebody to tell you to shower once in a while?"

Marlow shifted in her seat and looked away, pretending to study the ply board that had been nailed across the window. She wondered how her husband was doing... well, her ex-husband. And her two children. Molly would be a couple of years younger than the bratty kid about now...

"I don't suppose you do," said Dan offhandedly.

"You always this nice? Or is it a personality defect?" said Marlow through gritted teeth. "Especially to people trying to help you." She crossed over to the sealed window. Something about it was bugging her.

Dan didn't say another word. Marlow was pleased; it was about time somebody made the kid realise just how much he affected people around him.

She tapped the wood panels nailed across the window. It was a particularly thick piece. Now she knew what was bothering him.

"Your gramp's really serious about home security, ain't he? Nailed from the inside too. The bastard's trapped us in this room! Keep awake, least until I get a hammer and pull this thing off."

Marlow turned to leave the room. The first thing she noticed was that Dan was now asleep. The second thing was that a tapered black tentacle the size of the boy was oozing from under the bed. It moved with purpose; serrated spikes, sharp enough to decapitate a man, ran down either side of it. Four glowing red eyes blinked in rapid sequence from the darkness under the bed - a hunter's technique to ensure it always had three eyes open and its prey in sight.

Karkurium Nightmarus, recited Marlow from the pages she'd learnt as a child. This was the first time she'd seen one for real, and the waves of terror that pulsed from it made her legs wobble. She now regretted drawing a pair of glasses and a Groucho moustache on the hideous creature her grandpa had so carefully, and accurately drawn.

Marlow raised her gun. The tentacle swiped the barrel aside just as she pulled the trigger. There was a loud bang and the gun shot peppered the walls.

The limb swung back - tearing a sizeable gash in Marlow's coat and shirt beneath and knocking the weapon from her hand. She fell back against the chest of drawers, scattering books and comics. Several smaller tentacles whipped from the darkness with such fury that the bed bounced.

Unarmed, Marlow grabbed the chair she had been sitting on and swung it with all the force she could muster. It bounced harmlessly off two rubbery tentacles - a third wrapped around it and yanked it from her hand.

"Kid! Wake up! WHOA!" The last came as a yelp as a tentacle, this one with a barbed tip like a scorpion's stinger, punched towards her head. Marlow ducked just as it sank several inches into the plaster wall.

She jumped over another pair of tentacles snaking across the floor, these tipped with snapping beaks. She reached the bedroom door and was surprised to feel a trickle of guilt at leaving Dan alone with this thing, but she knew Infiltrators never harmed their Conduits.

The door was locked.

"What the...?"

Now she recalled a clicking sound as Boris had left them. The idiot had turned the key in the lock! Evidentially he didn't want Marlow to bail out, but had now trapped her in a room with no way of escape.

Marlow suddenly didn't feel sorry for Dan. She only felt sorry for herself.

The barbed limb slashed towards her. Marlow pushed flat against the wall and the spike missed her by inches before smashing through a thick door panel.

It was just what she needed. With a bellow, she charged the door, focusing her weight on the splintered wood. She felt a tentacle strike her back, but it only added to her momentum.

Marlow Cornelius flew headlong through the door and wood splintered all around her. Had she remembered the layout of the house, she would have handled her escape differently. The staircase was directly opposite Dan's room.

With a series of heavy thuds, Marlow landed halfway down the stairs and slid the rest of the way on her back, coming to rest in the Glass's hallway amid a pile of broken wood.

Boris and Bryony shot out of the living room. Marlow had demolished half the banister rails on her descent.

"Is it over with?" asked Boris, his eyes widening when he saw the blood seep through Marlow's coat.

Marlow saw it too, and winced when she touched the wound in her side. She was thinking of a caustic reply when a gurgling wet roar – like a slaughtered lion – came from upstairs as the Nightmare dragged itself from Dan's room.

The light dimmed around it as it sucked up photons, keeping it in a permanent pool of shadow, but the slug-like body that was visible was enough to cause Bryony to scream and Boris to faint.

"Go!" shouted Marlow as she pushed Bryony back into the living room. She grabbed Boris by the legs and dragged him in too.

In several seconds, Bryony had gone from hysterical to hyperventilating shock.

"The ones we've seen... have always been smaller..." she whispered between breaths.

Marlow didn't care. She dropped Boris' legs and slammed the door shut with her foot. She pushed the sofa across the door for added protection.

"Go to the kitchen and get me the biggest knife you can find."

Still exhibiting icy shock, Bryony nodded and ran into the kitchen which was fortunately accessible both through the dining room and the hall.

The living room door suddenly buckled as the beast rammed it from behind. Marlow lent her weight on the sofa to keep it in place.

"Hurry!"

With a jolt that shook the walls, the living room door fell off its hinges, and the sofa - with Marlow still on it - was hurled towards the large TV.

Her head cracked the screen which continued relentlessly playing Bryony's soap opera. Marlow was dazed, but Bryony's scream was enough for her to twist around so that she could see the Infiltrator fill the doorway, absorbing the light that came from the lights on the Christmas tree. Now it had moved, Marlow could make out something that wasn't on her Grandpa's illustrations - a circular mouth of razor-sharp teeth that spun around in its jaw like a blender. Tentacles oozed around the creature's body as it seeped into the room.

Bryony stood at the kitchen door holding the entire cutlery draw.

"Give me a knife!" shouted Marlow desperately. "Any knife!"

At least some rational part of Bryony's mind was functioning, and she threw the entire drawer at Marlow. Fortunately it landed short so Marlow didn't have to avoid any flying blades. She reached for the implements as a tentacle wrapped around her leg and began pulling her towards the mouth.

"Argh! Get off!" she used her untethered leg to kick the rubbery appendage, but it had no effect. Her fingers found what she was looking for, and she swung the knife into the heart of the beast.

It bounced off the hide.

Marlow looked at the blade incredulously, wondering just how blunt it was. *Very*, was the answer.

She was dragged across the floor so quickly that her coat and shirt rode up, and the skin on her exposed bare back suffered carpet burn. She whimpered with pain, but the approaching teeth promised a whole new world of agony.

The limb hoisted Marlow so high off the ground she felt her foot press against the ceiling as the Infiltrator angled her above its gyrating jaw. It gave its gurgle-roar again and Marlow could smell rancid decomposing fish.

Out of sheer desperation, rather than a preconceived plan, she stabbed the blunt knife into one of the Nightmare's four blood-red eyes. With a piercing scream, the creature suddenly released her as a foul slime sprayed out of the injured eye under high pressure.

Marlow landed on her head, and for a moment she blacked out. When she came to only seconds could have passed but the Nightmare had gone.

Bryony continued to scream.

Marlow clambered to her feet, noticing that there wasn't a single part of her that didn't hurt. She quickly fished a meat cleavers from the upturned draw and, ignoring Bryony's continuous single-note wail, edged into the hallway expecting the nightmare to ambush her.

Wallpaper ripped and pictures where torn from hooks. Sapphire coloured slime covered the walls from where the beast had pressed against it, but it had vanished.

Then Marlow noticed Dan at the top of the stairs, looking at the destruction with wide eyes.

"What did I miss?"

CHAPTER FOUR

"*THAT'S IT, luv. Just a little closer.*"

Marlow felt her father's hand shove her nearer to the slavering mouth. She was sure there was a solid bodied creature there, but all she could see was a mass of gnashing teeth and spittle yards away. Even at eight years old, she thought it was an extreme way of learning a new skill, but her father had assured her this was how she'd best learn the family business.

Marlow raised the heavy sword with both hands. Despite her regular circuit training, press-ups and stomach crunches before school, she could barely lift the dense Japanese katana blade, which her father swore was a family heirloom carved from a meteor. Ideal for slaying Nightmares.

"Lift it higher, luv. It'll soon as kill ya as give ya a chance to hurt it. Look for its weak spot - remember the Book!"

Marlow grunted with effort as she tried to lift the blade. The Infiltrator sensed her uncertainty and could certainly taste her fear, which her father had assured tasted metallic and bitter. It shot out a clawed fist that landed firmly in Marlow's stomach. She dropped the sword and rolled over in agony.

She hated the hunting business and swore, when she grew up, she'd have no part in it. Instead, she closed her eyes and tried to block out the sounds of her father slaying the beast while yelling at Marlow for being a coward. That was the first rib she had ever broken.

MARLOW OPENED HER EYES. She was in the shower, and it was twenty-nine years later. She never dreamed, or even daydreamed, but she could recall childhood memories better than recent ones, watching them play over her mind's eye in high-fidelity. It was a pity they were all bad.

She had broken pretty much every other bone since then and had become a dab hand at stitching up wounds as the network of scars across her body testified to. The very latest was the one across her abdomen from the night before. It still stung.

The telephone rang, its old speaker buzzing from the effort. She toyed with not answering it in case it was another job. They had become quite frequent as of late, which she put down to the fact word about her services was spreading since moving online. If it was a job it would mean more pain, but at least she would get paid. And now more than ever she needed the cash, especially with Christmas looming. She still hadn't bought her kids anything; something they expected from their loser of a mother.

Marlow grabbed a towel and ran into the living room, leaving soggy footprints in the carpet. She snatched the phone up.

"Marlow Cornelius."

"So I dialled the correct number then?" came the sneering voice on the other end of the line. There was only one person who could cram so much sarcasm in such few words: her ex-husband Trebor. How she ever fell for a guy with such a dumb name, she didn't know. "Hello Tree."

"Don't call me that," he snapped. "You know I don't like it."

"Sorry, Tree." She could hear the intake of breath as he resisted taking the bait.

"I've been trying to call you all day."

"Congratulations, you figured out how to dial a number. I'll send you a badge. How are the kids?" The words felt like lead in her mouth. She hadn't seen her children for at least two years because Trebor always conveniently engineered them all too busy when she was free. When they had decided to get a divorce, she knew that it would affect the children. It must be horrible to have your parents split up; and, as one of the parents, she wasn't thrilled about it either.

"It's Jamie's birthday this weekend," said Trebor. Marlow perked up - she'd forgotten about that. It was too close to Christmas to stay in her memory. Could this finally be the invite she had longed for? "And I want to make sure you are nowhere near us at the time."

"Tree, I want to see my children."

"They don't want to see you." The words were a dagger in her chest. Marlow knew that if her kids wanted nothing to do with her, then she should at least hear it from them. However, it was difficult to sustain her indignation; she was afraid that Trebor was telling the truth. "I will, however, expect you to send money over for a present. And for their Christmas presents too."

Marlow sighed. Almost everything she earned was sent to her children, or more correctly, to Trebor. She just hoped that he was spending it on them.

"Sure."

"Good. I will expect it soon."

Trebor hung up before she could object. Marlow gently placed the phone down and stared into space. She'd once had the perfect marriage, and they had been blessed with two wonderful children: Jamie and Molly. Despite her upbringing, she had hoped that her life was about to change for the better. But it was not to be. One night Trebor had discovered the true nature of her job, a fact she had shamefully kept from him for years. He gave her little chance to explain, terrified that their children would fall victim of some abdominal creature she would bring home. Tree had promptly thrown her out. Marlow knew the subsequent divorce was her own fault. She had lied from the very beginning of their relationship and she hated herself for that, but there was no way to un-sow a lie. And when it came to explaining herself during the divorce proceedings, the truth would only brand her insane.

Marlow sat back on the threadbare sofa, not caring that she was still wet. Life wasn't fair; she couldn't even see her children in her dreams and had a difficult time recalling their faces even now.

Why was it she only remembered the bad things so clearly?

DAN LOOKED around his hotel room. It was quite large with a double bed, an en suite bathroom, a small uncomfortable sofa, a coffee table, a TV and kettle, which was already on the boil. He was impressed that the Travel Stop was so well appointed considering most people only ever spent one night in it.

His parents had fled the house almost straight after Marlow had departed. The hotel was a twenty minutes ride away, and on arriving, his Mum and Grandpa had left him there alone and returned to fix up their home the best they could.

Dan was still shaking after witnessing the destruction

around his house, but didn't understand how he could be responsible for it. He upturned his backpack, spilling the contents on the bed, containing anything he could hastily grab: some crumpled comics, a book about ninjas, his mobile phone, an extra big coffee mug, and a semi-melted chocolate bar.

Suspicious as to why the weird woman had been called in to help, he had discreetly hidden the mobile amongst the clutter of his bedroom. He wanted to see for himself what these monsters looked like.

His mother had given him several energy drinks, none of which he touched as their taste was beginning to make him feel nauseous. The last time he'd drank three, one-after-the-other, he'd hallucinated for hours that mice with capes and masks were running around his house acting as superheroes. Right now, the shock at the wreckage back home was more than enough to keep him awake.

How could being asleep do all that damage? He couldn't seriously believe the story about the monsters. Still, he'd read ghost stories about people plagued by poltergeist, and for a couple of years he had suspected that's what was causing the disturbances in his bedroom. They were just minor things: things knocked over, windows and doors cracked opened from the inside, drawers left ajar, their contents strewn across the floor. It had been worrying, but nothing to concern his Mum or Grandpa about. They were much more concerned with his narcolepsy. He had often complained about it, but it was only when he had been riding his bike and fell asleep at the handle-bars, thus sleep-peddling across a busy traffic junction, that they decided enough was enough and sought professional medical help.

That had been a waste of time. He' d been wired to machines and had had his brainwaves analysed. He tried numerous tablets, experimental drugs, vitamin shots, aromatherapy, stringent exercise - nothing had worked. The doctors had declared that he would finally grow out of it - which was their way of saying 'we're drawing a blank, so don't ask us anymore!'

Dan made himself a double strength coffee, just in case, then sat down cross-legged on the bed and opened his mobile's video app. He put the pillows behind his back, including the extra ones he had found stashed in the wardrobe, and got comfortable.

He pressed play on the video. On the screen the familiar image of his bedroom appeared as he adjusted the camera and darted to his bed. Dan scrubbed through the footage until he saw Marlow enter the room and sit just out of view.

He gripped his hot coffee with both hands and watched the tiny screen intently...

MARLOW AWOKE WITH A START. For once the phone was silent, which was no surprise because she had yanked it from the wall during the night. The first thing she saw was the full wine bottle on the table – and felt a tremor of pride that she had resisted touching it. However, the two other empty bottles that rolled from her legs as she sat up proved that her willpower hadn't been so strong after all. She scratched her head - then stopped. There was that noise again. It was coming from the front door.

With a wheeze, Marlow pulled herself from the sofa and slowly crossed to the door. She couldn't remember the last time anybody had knocked on it. Hesitating, she cranked it open a couple of inches. Boris Glass stared at her with puffy red eyes.

"Oh, no..." Marlow turned away, a silent offer for Boris to enter the apartment. "How d'you find me?"

"I work for the Council. I pulled every string I could to track you down, since your phone isn't working."

"Yeah, it does that sometimes."

Marlow crossed to the open-plan kitchen and wrestled with the tarnished tap to pour herself a pint of water into an unwashed glass. She drank it in one go, wincing from the grim taste.

"I did everything I could last night," Marlow said, immediately on the defensive. "You're not getting a penny back."

"Dan–"

"Dan is weird, I grant you," Marlow regretted her choice of words, but it was out there now.

"But–"

"Conduits can bring them things through twice a week, three, tops. And that was a very unusual case. A little girl, bad breath, awful taste in music - but anyway, it can't happen after the Infiltrator's been killed. So your boy hosted a new Infiltrator. That's pretty far from normal. Two nightmares and a daymare in two days? I don't know what to say. There's not much I can do about that."

"You're the only one who can handle this kind of thing!"

"I'm sure there are others." She knew that was a lie, or at least if there were they didn't advertise their services and her father had never spoken of them. "Not that they will be as good as me," she added, just in case.

"Miss Cornelius..."

"Call me Marlow. Nobody calls me Miss. And Cornelius I don't like the sound of." It reminded her of her father and the further she could get away from that connection, the better.

"We have a very big problem."

"Yeah, we do. You want a refund and I won't be issuing it. Sorry."

"Dan has gone missing!"

"Then problem solved." The words had come out before the implications of what Boris was saying had a chance to weigh in. "Wait, missing?"

Marlow pushed her scrappy fringe from her eyes to get a better look at Boris. Her first assumption that he was tired was only half true. Boris wore the look of a man on the edge of his sanity.

"Yes. *Missing.* We need your help."

MARLOW LOOKED around the Travel Stop hotel room, searching for clues. Aside from a stack of pillows, the bed hadn't been slept in. She tried the window; it was locked from the inside. An over-sized coffee mug sat next to the TV, the contents only half finished.

Boris stood at the door, not daring to enter.

"Bryony has stayed at the house, just in case he turns up there."

Marlow could see no telltale signs of Infiltrator action: no trails of dried slime, no claw marks, no pulverised furniture, and absolutely no blood.

"There's no evidence here that They got him."

"Then where is he?"

Marlow's hangover rattled when Boris spoke loudly. She gestured that he should lower his volume a tad.

"Infiltrators don't take people. They eat people, sure. Kill them without a second thought, absolutely - but abduct them? Nah."

"Then where is he?"

"Your grandson is a Conduit. For them, that's a very rare thing to have access to, and in Dan's case it looks like he is some kind of Super-Conduit between worlds. There's no way they would have harmed such a precious resource."

Boris looked around the room with increasing despair.

A glint from under the sofa caught Marlow's attention. She stooped to investigate, sliding out a cracked screen mobile phone that had almost vanished under it. She picked it up, thumbing the power button. Dead.

"That's his!" gasped Boris, snatching it from her hand.

Marlow suspected what had happened. He wouldn't be the first kid to record what went on in the dead of night. She sighed deeply and was surprised to feel a pang of sorrow. She didn't know with whom she was sympathising with more: Boris or Dan.

"Dan hasn't been taken. He ran away."

"No. He would never leave it behind. They must have taken him!"

"When you charge this up, look at the videos. I bet that's what Dan did. He recorded our last encounter."

Boris's jaw worked silently for a moment. When he spoke again his voice was nothing more than a hoarse whisper. "You must find him for us. Please." The last word was a physical effort.

Marlow felt a swell of emotions she usually slayed with alcohol. This case was getting much too personal for her tastes.

"I can't do that, you need to tell the cops."

"Tell them what?" hissed Boris. "That my Grandson has run away because monsters came out of his nightmares and destroyed our house? Do you really think they will believe me? His mother and I will be carted off to prison or the asylum!" He was getting increasingly hysterical.

Every instinct told Marlow to walk away. A runaway was a police problem, not hers. The golden rule, or one of them, was never to get involved with a customer. She would just have to block dark thoughts of Dan's fate from her mind and move on with her own life. Devoured by monsters was just one of those curve balls light threw at you.

Instead, she took the phone from Boris' hand and stared at it for a long moment. Then she nodded and was shocked to find herself saying: "OK. I'll find him for ya."

CHAPTER FIVE

THE MOST SURPRISING THING, Dan thought, was that the word 'impossible' had faded from his vocabulary, to be replaced with the more mundane 'how?', 'why?' and 'huh?'.

After settling into the hotel room, he'd watched the video recording four times. During each playback his shaking finger scrubbed the footage back to the moment Marlow had been hurled through the door and the monster chased her. No, not chase, 'flowed after her' was a better description. The beast moved as if it had been swimming and the shadows were nothing more than deep ocean waters.

Never once did Dan question the validity of the footage. He knew computer graphics could create the most amazing special effects, but he also knew this was no setup. Marlow hadn't created the footage and sneaked it onto his phone. What he was watching was the real deal. He accepted that without question.

Then he must have fallen asleep as he stared at a still image of a particularly frightening shot of the creature's slavering jaw, the glass-like slender teeth catching what little light was in the room. He couldn't be sure how long he'd slept, he suspected seconds. But when he awoke, the room had been trashed and the screen on his phone shattered. That's when his instinct to flee kicked in. Even if he was trying to run from himself.

With his heart thumping, he had tidied the room as best he could and bolted.

Marlow's explanation of his freaky power replayed through his mind. Of course he hadn't believed her. Only when his Grandpa wheeled him to the Travel Stop had he wondered if there were any grains of truth in the crazy woman's words. His Grandpa had left with an odd look on his face; a cross between fear and an apology, and had whispered: *"It's not my fault,"* before he left. To Dan, that proved beyond a doubt that his Grandpa and Mother were genuinely frightened; *frightened of him.* Too fearful to have the freak stay any longer under their roof. Dan now saw that dropping him in the Travel Stop was the only solution they had to get rid of him.

But that wouldn't stop the nightmares. Dan no longer had doubts that he was on his own. He was solely responsible for the manifestations and staying here, in a full hotel, simply put more people at risk when he slept.

And he slept a lot.

He disappeared into the night with only his backpack and a few hastily gathered chocolate bars and packets of crisps from the hotel lobby's vending machine, using every coin he possessed. He'd ran with no regard notion of a destination, just the absolute belief that everybody in the Travel Stop, not to mention his family, would be better off if he was gone.

The hotel was on the outskirts of the town near a sprawling industrial park of newly built glass and stone build-ings that housed trendy design companies, a couple of eco businesses, one of which made wind farm turbines, and other nameless companies that meant nothing to Dan. The only thing he knew with certainty was that the road he was treading led to a large roundabout and was marked by the last petrol station for several miles. Branching roads lead to dark A-roads that cut through the surrounding countryside, and the motorway leading to the rest of the world.

He supposed that if he didn't have a destination in mind then none of them could be the wrong direction. He hoisted his backpack further onto his shoulders, suppressed a tearful choke at the thought of never seeing his family again, and marched purposefully towards the roundabout.

Five minutes later, Dan tumbled down a ditch, rolling end-over-end through sharp brambles – and crumpled to a halt, completely fast asleep.

RAVI KAFFORAN STUDIED THE TEXTBOOK, filled with complex engineering equations, but under his keen gaze they unravelled into tensions and strains denoting the load a hypothetical bridge could handle. In his last year of his engineering degree, it was a discipline that suited him perfectly. He liked things to fit into neat boxes and had a passion for logic and order, after all, his lecturers had drilled into him that *'numbers are what makes the world go around.'*

He glanced up as the petrol pump control panel binged for attention. There was a rough-looking skinhead on pump six who had the hose inserted into his pimped up boy-racer car and was drumming his fingers impatiently on the roof while glaring at Ravi through the thick glass. He said some-thing to the two other brutish occupants in the car and sniggered.

Ravi double-checked the surveillance camera was recording the forecourt and had digitally logged the licence plate, a precaution against drivers who decide to fill up and go without paying. Satisfied, he activated the pump, and the skinhead started filling his car.

The night shift always brought potential danger. It seemed the scum of the earth always emerged when the light fell, but Ravi needed the job. After the year and a half he'd been doing the twilight shifts he had grown quite adept at reading people - and the skinhead looked like trouble. Probably not the type to try to rob him, but the right breed of moron to take pleasure in verbally abusing him. He checked the main door was locked, which meant the skinhead would be forced to pay over the night counter, served him right for choosing to dress like a creep.

Ravi focused on the problem in his book. His fingers rattled across the buttons on his phone's scientific calculator App as he worked out the problem. He was so immersed in the equation that he jumped when a fist hammered against the bulletproof cashier's window. He looked up to see the skinhead pounding the glass. At first he assumed his expression was the usual look of stupidity, anger and hatred - then he realised the skinhead was terrified of something. What that something was, Ravi couldn't see because the entire forecourt was bathed in darkness. The canopy lights were on, but they were smothered as if a thick black fog was sucking up the illumination. He could only just make out the skinhead's car - and the occupants who were falling over each other in their desperation to clamber from the passenger door.

Ravi watched in astonishment as the vehicle rocked as it was hammered into from the side. Even through the thick glass he could hear the thugs inside wailing. The Skinhead stopped pounding on the glass and turned to follow Ravi's horrified gaze.

Black tentacles, the size of oak trees ruptured from the darkness and coiled around the vehicle. The two passengers almost made it out before the car lifted into the air at such an angle that they fell back inside - the door slamming shut, trapping them. The powerful snaking limbs hoisted the car into the darkness.

Ravi winced when the sound of rendering metal echoed across the forecourt and the car came slamming down with such force it rolled into the petrol pumps, crushing the thin metal cases and severing the feeder pipes inside. Clear fluid flooded across the forecourt.

But Ravi's brain wasn't concerned with the pooling fuel. His eyes were fixed on the car as it continued rolling, thrown by some immense force. The roof had been peeled back like a sardine can. Bitten back, Ravi corrected himself when he noticed that the serrated metal looked as if a shark had taken a mouthful. There was no sign of the occupants.

The Skinhead looked pleadingly back at Ravi. Ravi reached for the door release - but he was too late. Like a whip, a black coil shot around the Skinhead's waist and yanked him backward into the pitch black.

Ravi backpedalled away from the window like a startled rabbit. His senses kicked in and he noticed the sickly smell of petrol fumes as the fuel bubbled up in a fountain from the petrol tanks buried below.

The darkness pressed against the glass like a fog bank, causing his view of the forecourt to fade like the end shot of a movie. He pressed further into the shop and then ran for the far door which was the only appropriate place he could think of: the restroom.

With shaking hands, Ravi slammed the door shut and locked it. Then he sat on the toilet seat and prayed that he was dreaming.

. . .

ONCE MARLOW'S brain had caught up with her mouth she had tried to backpedal from agreeing to help find Dan, after all, locating missing people was not her forte. However, Boris refused to listen and profusely kept thanking her.

To save face, Marlow suggested Boris first go to the police and report Dan missing. Boris had railed against the idea.

"They'll think we are terrible parents!" gushed Boris. "He'll be taken from his mother and placed into care. Is that what you want?" Marlow didn't want anything except the problem to go away. Boris had continued laying the guilt. "And then they'll get a psychologist to analyse him. What do you think a shrink would do if he heard such nonsensical tales of living nightmares? The boy would be locked away in a padded room and studied for the rest of his life. We can't allow that to happen!"

After minutes of agonising guilt, Marlow held up her hand to shut him up. "OK, enough! I hear you, but in that case we should talk about my fee."

Marlow felt a rare twinge of guilt talking about money; God knows she was always looking for an angle to increase her fees. But here was a young boy, lost in the world with no idea of what he was capable of, and Marlow was figuring how to profit from the situation. Only by thinking about her own children, at least how she remembered them, and the harpy call of her Ex demanding money, lessened the guilt.

A daily fee was agreed, plus expenses, and Boris left, insisting that Marlow contact him every six hours to inform him of progress, or lack of. Marlow had hurried to her Beetle and slammed the door closed, thankful for a few minutes of isolation. She breathed hard, wondering what she had got herself tangled up in.

The rest of the day passed quickly. There was little point in driving around the city looking for Dan. If the boy wanted to fall off the radar, then Marlow doubted he would be stupid enough to draw attention to himself, and if he was, then perhaps the police would pick him up and solve Marlow's problem. She just hoped to rack up a day or two of fees before that happened. She reasoned the best cause of action was to return home and keep monitoring the news for any unusual incidents that might indicate that Dan had passed by. Strange black cats, chupacabra, weird lights in the sky - something subtle that would allow only the most knowledgeable to suspect what was really amiss. She turned on the TV and thumbed through the usual morning dross until she found a local news channel.

"Police are still baffled as to why the petrol station exploded," read a newsreader calmly.

Marlow hunched down in front of the screen as footage showed the fire brigade tackling the smouldering embers of the petrol station.

The Newsreader continued. "The local man on duty at the time, student Ravi Kafforan, survived the blast and claimed a group of teenagers had arrived just minutes before."

The picture changed to a young Indian man who was being escorted to an ambulance by a policewoman. He clutched a bandage to his head as his wild eyes scanned the emergency crews. As soon as he saw the camera he surged towards them.

"It came from the darkness! It got them! It got them!" he babbled before the officer steered him back towards the ambulance, a firm arm around his shoulders preventing him from talking to the camera.

The picture changed back to the Newsreader. "Police say he was fortunate to only be suffering from mild-head trauma and hoped to interview him later today for more details. In other news..."

Marlow muted the rest of the report. She knew the petrol

station; it was the one on the edge of town, near the motorway. It was too much of a coincidence for it not to be linked to Dan, but the sheer scale of the devastation... a shiver ran through her. Infiltrators disrupted homes, ate a few dogs, on occasion caused minor property damage but never caused destruction on a scale like this.

Her mind went back to the incident in school. At the time she hadn't known it was linked to Dan, so had only half watched the reports. But thinking back, the damage the nightmarish ape had caused was far from usual. The thing back in Dan's house had been powerful too...

"Focus," Marlow whispered to herself. She reasoned that Dan was heading out of town. The kid was smart. He could easily hitch a ride on the motorway and get far away with the minimal of fuss. The question was, which direction was he heading?

Marlow moved to her supply closet, filled with firearms, baseball bats in various states of wear, and a sword she liked the look of and had purchased from a second-hand shop. She tested the blade; it was blunt and therefore useless, not like the sword her father had carried.

Her father... Marlow did everything she could to resist taking over the family business, but her father had been adamant it had to be her. Sure, he would have preferred a son, but he was out of luck in that department. Marlow's older sister, Gina, was now a florist somewhere in Scotland. They never really stayed in touch, especially after she married. Like all of Marlow's personal relationships, it had just faded away as she reluctantly stepped into her father's shoes. Gina could dream and, as children, she had regaled Marlow with stories of her dreams; far-off places she could never visit. Marlow had always resented her dreamless nights, but her father had taken it as a sign that she was a bona fide nightmare hunter, destined to continue the family tradition, while her sister was resigned to a normal life.

Marlow hated him. She wished she could tell him to his face, but that would never happen.

With a regretful sigh, Marlow cast those thoughts aside and pulled an aging chunky radio scanner from the cupboard. The aerial snagged several times as she extended it. She couldn't recall the last time it was used and wondered if it would still work. The power switch tried to resist being pushed in, but she was rewarded with a flickering green power light. She placed it on the table, cranked up the volume and set the controls to 'scan'. It was already illegally tuned into police radio frequencies from a previous endeavour, but Marlow figured they were all working on the same side whether or not they knew it. She unmuted the TV and set it to a rolling national news channel. If Dan had travelled far, then the police scanner would be useless, and the national news network would provide her only sourced of intel. It was a lazy approach, but all she could think of.

With a deep sigh, Marlow settled back on the lumpy sofa and closed her eyes to listen.

DAN'S RUMBLING stomach woke him. At first he thought he was back at home on his uncomfortable mattress until a gorse bush scratched his cheek and he sat bolt upright in the ditch.

Memories of the last twenty-four hours came flooding back as he squinted in the morning sunlight. His backpack was still firmly attached, his left foot damp from where it had landed in the full drainage ditch, but otherwise he was fine. The question was where was he? Anywhere but home, he thought as the image of his mother crying, his Grandpa draping a consoling

arm around her and whispering that it was for the best Dan
had vanished.

He whipped off his wet trainer and damp sock. Wringing it
dry, his knuckles turned white as he assaulted it using all his
pent-up anger. He slipped it back on, then fished a Mars bar
from his pack, tore the wrapper open and shovelled it greedily
down. He immediately regretted the fact he had chosen to dry
his mangy footwear off first, as his hands now smelled
disgusting and the chocolate didn't taste much better.
Resisting the urge to spit it out, Dan swallowed it – almost
choking. He chased the taste away with a fizzy energy drink
and was glad he'd took time to raid the hotel's vending
machine before he left. Maybe not the healthiest meal, but
with his lifespan currently critically low, it would at least keep
him awake.

It was cold and the morning sky above was blue, but leaden
clouds were already threatening the horizon. Hooking his
thumbs in the straps of his pack, Dan set off towards the
motorway. After several minutes he reached the roundabout,
broadening his line of sight beyond the trees edging it. A flare
of lights forced him to duck into the bushes at the side of the
road, ignoring the sharp branches scratching his skin. His gaze
was fixed on the cordon of police cars and fire engines
surrounding the petrol station.

What used to be the petrol station, he corrected himself.

It was now just a jagged mass of twisted black metal and
concrete. A car lay on its roof, in the centre of the forecourt.
The fender savagely smashed in. He presumed it had crashed,
causing the fire. As usual, another spectacular thing he'd
missed. He hoped nobody had been hurt in the inferno, but it
must have looked cool.

The presence of the police gave him cause to pause. Would
his Grandpa notice he was missing yet? A quick glance at his

watch showed it was nine thirty. He had slept heavily through the night. Then an ominous thought struck him... had *he* caused the fire? Had a fire-breathing dragon soared out of his dreams and torched the place? He shivered, surely not... but if anything, it strengthened his resolve to leave everybody he cared for behind.

Dan cut through the bushes. They were dense and tangles of brier snagged his foot, forcing him to flail his way through. It took several minutes to circumnavigate the petrol station and emerge onto the motorway slip road.

A quick glance at a road sign revealed the stretch of road headed north. He had no clear idea of his final destination, so north was as good as any other compass point. He stretched out his arm, raising his thumb in the international sign of a hitchhiker.

A dozen cars slid up the entrance ramp and onto the motorway without so much as slowing for him. A couple blared their horns, and it occurred to Dan that people might not stop to pick up a kid trying to hitch a ride.

A sleek red sports car roared past, followed by a pair of blue Mercedes, a van, a motorbike... like counting sheep, Dan thought as his eyelids started to feel heavy. How long had it been since he had fuelled himself with caffeine? Thirty minutes? An hour? Longer? Staying awake for more than an hour at a stretch was a huge effort without regular doses of caffeine to keep him on his toes.

Maybe just a quick shut eye...

NO! Dan screamed inwardly. He couldn't fall asleep. Not here. Not now. He refused to let that happen. He had prac-tised controlling his sleep disorder with sheer willpower, but unfortunately it seldom worked, instead it just sank him deeper into the welcoming arms of Morpheus.

Morpheus... what had Maven told him? The Greek God of dreams? The name sounded fat and comfortable...

Dan felt himself sliding forwards, ever so gently, as if riding a giant feather to the ground. All exterior noise faded into a quiet hum.

Then something stirred. Something on the edge of his vision. His mind's eye fought to focus on it but his gaze kept sliding off. It was a large creature. Dan could just make out the multiple legs as it galloped towards him. Silver fangs lined an impossibly big mouth that stretched open with a deep–

HHHOOOONNKKK!!

Dan jerked awake - only to discover that he was toppling into the road as a huge articulated lorry bore down on him. The truck filled his vision. The horn was deafening, but not quite loud enough to drown out the squeal of rubber as the brakes on all eighteen wheels locked and rubber burned.

Like a collection of snapshots, Dan saw the Volvo logo mounted on the lorry's grill grow larger. He picked out the full licence plate in perfect detail - every letter and number filled his field of vision with Imax-like force.

Dan tried to move - but fell flat on his backside.

The lorry ground to a halt inches from crushing him. The Driver jumped from the cab, eyes scanning the road ahead. "Oh my God! Oh my God!" he repeated like a mantra. "Christ, son! Are you OK?"

Dan stood and wobbled on his heels. "I'm fine," he said batting the Driver's helping hand aside as he reached to stop Dan from falling again.

"Don't move. I'll call an ambulance."

"No need," said Dan, stifling a yawn despite the near death experience he had just experienced.

Seeing that the boy was alive, in perfect health, tired and

bad tempered, the Driver's concern evaporated and was replaced with recrimination.

"What the hell where you trying to do? Walking out in the road like that?"

"Actually, I was falling asleep." The explanation only served to baffle the man. Dan gave him a broad smile that further disarmed the Driver's sense of outrage. "Anyway, thanks for stopping! I would've been waiting *hours* out here, I reckon."

Without waiting for an invitation, Dan leapt up into the lorry's cab and shuffled along to the passenger's side. The Driver was nonplussed as angry horns honked behind him. Taking several paces back, he saw the long line of traffic backing up on the roundabout, blocked by his lorry. He jumped into the cab and stared at the boy as he dropped his backpack in the footwell and pulled the seatbelt on.

"What do you think you're doing?" he asked impatiently.

"Buckling up. Safety first."

"I meant in my cab? Get out."

"I was hitchhiking. Didn't you see my thumb? I thought that's why you stopped?"

"You were falling into the road!"

Dan mustered all the innocence he could convey. "Really? Oh, silly me. I'm so sorry if it looked that way." The irritating medley of horns behind them agitated the Driver. Dan tried to keep the smile off his face and looked as forlorn as possible. "Well, if you think it was an accident we must tell the police, although I don't want you getting into trouble. And to think I was hoping to get to my Grandpa's before it got too dark." He slowly extended a hand for the door handle. "Such a shame. He's so ill…"

The Driver's gaze switched between Dan and the side mirror, and a sea of furious heads poking from windows to see what the problem was. The mention of police had ruffled him.

Since the boy was unharmed police intervention would not only make him late for his deliveries but also give his boss an excuse to berate him and study the lorry's tachograph, which recorded every detail of the journey: each time he stopped, his speed, everything. A careful analysis would highlight his penchant for speeding, which would give him a black mark on his licence. He quickly made his mind up and snapped his seatbelt on before Dan could open the door. He hadn't even noticed that Dan hadn't taken his seatbelt off.

"OK, OK, no harm done. Let's go." He put the lorry into gear and they lurched forward. "Where were you heading?"

Dan's mind raced. He hadn't given a thought to his destination. He needed some texture to smooth the lie. "Scotland. Edinburgh, to see my Grandpa."

"I'm not going that far. I'll drop you off along the way." They merged onto the motorway, a long precession of vehicles behind them. Now they were moving, the Driver's suspicions started to kick in. "Why are you hitchhiking to Scotland? Where are your parents?"

Dan yawned. As he stared out of the windshield, the lies came fluently. "I live with my younger brother. Our parents are dead and Grandpa's ill. We didn't have enough money for the train, so I decided to hitchhike." Each word came out smoothly but slowly. The gentle rocking of the lorry and monotonous thrum of the engine was lulling him to sleep.

The Driver said something, but it was lost in the warm hum that enveloped Dan as he slipped away...

He suddenly bit his tongue so hard that he jolted awake. There was a taste of blood in his mouth and he winced from the pain, but the technique had served him well a couple of times when he had fought his narcoleptic choke. He blinked rapidly and took a deep breath, hoping that the oxygen would ignite his brain enough to keep him awake a little longer.

"It would be great if we could stop at the next service station," said Dan. "I could do with a coffee and I think I owe you one by way of thanks."

The Driver gave a quick sidelong glance at his passenger. There was something odd about the boy, but he just couldn't put his finger on it. With any luck he would fall asleep before they reached the next service station so he could drive past. He couldn't afford any more unscheduled stops.

CHAPTER SIX

ONERISM HAD MANY ANNOYING ATTRIBUTES, but one of the most irritating, at least on a daily basis for Marlow, was that because her dreams were replaced by blackness - utter darkness as if she were blindfolded in a windowless underground room at the zenith of midnight - it came with no sense of time. That was the condition Marlow had suffered all her life and she long ago wished a card would appear in her imagination with the words 'insert scene here'. At least she could read the sign over-and-over to give her some sense of the passage of time.

Instead the seconds, minutes, hours all blended into a void that was nothing more than an overly long blinking of the eye. One moment it could be sunset, the next blink it was midday, and she was feeling refreshed, even if a sliver of congealed drool usually clung to the corner of her mouth.

It happened while Marlow was listening to the police scanner. This particular catnap was even more unwelcome because she had not been aware she'd fallen asleep until she glanced at her grubby diver's watch, a rare gift from her father, and noticed that two hours had mysteriously vanished. Vexed, she scanned the news for any signs of unusual activity but found nothing. In the two hours she had slept, Dan could have made it far away.

So far away that he was no longer my problem, an inner devil whispered.

Marlow shooed that thought away. Even though she was jealous that Dan could so readily, and vividly dream, she felt some sympathy for the kid. Only a tinge, mind.

With nothing more that to do, and certain that Boris Glass would soon be banging on her door again, Marlow decided to get out of her apartment. At least the air would be fresher outside as something had gone off in the fridge and Marlow hadn't drummed up the courage to investigate what it was. Fighting nightmare monsters was one thing, but wilfully touching some mouldy alien growth in the fridge - the mere thought churned her stomach.

Marlow climbed into her Volkswagen Beetle that was now more rust than machine, and, after turning the engine four times and keeping the accelerator floored to flood the engine, it coughed to life. She had intended to head to a local Starbucks to get something to perk her up. The one advantage with her appearance was that she easily got a table for herself at such establishments; sometimes she could claim a whole booth as her own territory. Even the tramps on the street didn't bother her; never once had she been hassled for spare change - and once, she had even been taken aside by a thin wastrel and told where she could find a free soup kitchen. Being hard up on cash at the time, she had gone with it.

Musing over her terrible life choices, Marlow was surprised to find that she had been driving on autopilot towards her ex-husband's house. Or, as she used to call it, *her home*. She considered performing a U-turn and sticking to her plan, but some inner tractor beam drew her nearer.

Familiar street signs started to appear and the neighbour-hood became markedly more upmarket with each passing street. Ah, those were the days...

She turned into the street - her old street, that is - and received a few suspicious looks from various residents who had decided that today was the day to tend their front gardens. Undisguised disparaging looks – from the very people she once knew as neighbours, who now didn't recognise the wreck she had become - made it clear that she wasn't welcome in their little patch of heaven.

Marlow stopped several houses away from her old haunt. She let the engine idle and watched several children play in the street outside her ex-home.

Was that Molly and Jamie amongst them? It had been so long and they must have grown so much... Christ, what was wrong with her that she couldn't even recognise her *own* children? She was *sure* it was them...

The youths booted a ball around with reckless abandon, and their shrieks of laughter broke through the throaty rattle of her jalopy. She wanted to climb out and wave, but feared they would take one look at her and flee in terror. That's if they remembered her at all.

The football swerved in a graceful arc and thumped against the bonnet so hard it left a dent.

Marlow panicked as the children turned towards her. For a split second she studied their faces and kicked herself because she still couldn't recall which, if any, were her own.

It's been too long.

Gears ground as she put the Beetle into reverse and hit the accelerator, The car bounced from the curb and she pranged into a lamp post. The children were now looking at her with mouths hanging open in astonishment. Marlow dared not meet their gaze as she crunched into first gear and twisted the wheel so hard that the addled Volkswagen whined as it performed a sharp U-turn, balding tyres screeched in protest as they painted the road with a pair of black skid-marks. The gearbox barked as she tried to find second, so instead opted for third and a less speedy getaway.

Marlow's hands shook as she turned the police scanner back on. She noticed an old phone charger coiled amongst wrappers on the floor. She quickly pulled into a bus stop and retrieved it. Taking Dan's dead phone from her pocket, she checked if they matched: bingo. She quickly plugged the charger into the cigarette lighter and checked the phone was charging before she pulled away.

Back on the road her thoughts drifted once more. She berated herself, feeling stupid for the detour. Her family didn't want to see her, Trebor had made that very clear. A second later, a trickle of doubt rippled across those self-deprecating thoughts; had she misinterpreted him? Was he angry precisely because *she* had stayed away? It was difficult to judge, especially as her short-term memory was foggy at the best of time.

A police report caught her attention: something about a jackknifed lorry on the motorway. It wasn't unusual or out of the ordinary... but *something* nagged Marlow that she should at least investigate. It would be nothing other than a welcome distraction from her immediate problems. Glancing at her watch she realised she was overdue calling Boris with an update, and at least visiting the police emergency would prove she'd done something to look for his stupid grandson.

It took just under two hours for Marlow to get within viewing distance of the over-turned lorry. Traffic in both directions had severely backed up, resulting in jams that stretched for five miles and were still growing. The police siphoned traffic off the motorway, which resulted in severe congestion in the arterial roads around the area. In the end, Marlow had to park her car at the side of a B-road, clamber up a muddy embankment and walk across a footbridge that was crowded with gawkers. Every step of the way she was convinced it was a waste of time, but her nagging conscience about the fate of the kid propelled her on. That, plus the negotiated daily rate she had agreed with Boris, which was almost double her usual fee.

The spectators naturally parted when Marlow pressed through. Despite her shower, her clothes stank to high-heaven. The view before her was... *impressive* was the first word that came to mind. The next was: disastrous.

The lorry had jackknifed through the median barriers, tipping onto its side and sliding to a halt, blocking both lanes. As far as Marlow could tell, no other vehicle had been struck. Anything approaching from the opposite direction would have surely vaporised on impact. The lorry's load of electrical goods were strewn across the carriageway. Glancing behind her, Marlow could see the trail of destruction the fallen goods had caused. Several had claimed victims. One car had a boxed microwave through the windscreen while a minibus had collided with a fridge freezer with such force that the front of the vehicle had wrapped around it. A washing machine had caused several cars to veer aside - straight into the path of an overtaking 4x4 - while a pickup had winged the washing machine and spun one-hundred and eighty degrees.

She brought her gaze back to the truck itself. Something about it had sounded a note of alarm in the recesses of her mind, but only after twenty seconds of scrutinization did she consciously notice it.

The lorry's trailer had been shredded apart in a very particular fashion that was instantly recognisable to her. Petals of the metal container were peeled back in such a way she could envisage massive claws tearing it open from the inside. Now she knew what she was looking for, Marlow could see a jagged chunk of metal had been taken from the back of the lorry's roof. To the untrained eye it was just the result of the crash, but Marlow recognised a massive bite mark when she saw one.

With rising panic, she pushed her way through the growing crowd; many of the vultures were taking photographs on their phones. At the end of the bridge, she vaulted the rail and scrambled down the steep incline to the road. Her boots slipped and she tumbled uncontrollably down, landing on her back on the hard shoulder. Ignoring the ache, she dashed across the tarmac, towards one of several police officers surrounding the vehicle.

"Was anyone hurt?" Marlow demanded with as much authority as she could muster.

The Officer turned, his eyes widening when he saw what was approaching; his flaring nostrils followed suit. "You can't be here, miss."

"Can't I?" said Marlow, momentarily confused. "Well, I am, clearly. Was anyone hurt?"

The Officer wasn't prepared for her apparent incomprehension and had no desire to be in close proximity to escort her away, so he answered the second question.

"Few injuries. No fatalities. Bloody lucky escape all round. Driver had a few cuts 'n' bruises, and the same for the other drivers. Whiplash central it is. Anyway, you can't be on the motorway. Not allowed," he added in the hope the clarity would send Marlow back to whichever dump she had crawled from.

Marlow craned to look over the officer's shoulder. "A kid... was there a boy onboard?"

"A boy?" asked the Officer confused as to why Marlow was still looking at the wreckage with such concern.

"Yes," hissed Marlow impatiently, "A kid. A child. A boy. About yey big." She held up her hand to approximate Dan's height.

The Officer bristled. "I do know how big children tend to be, miss." The Officer's patience was thinning. Every day he was called out to traffic accidents, and they were never very pleasant affairs. This one was a lucky break with nobody killed, and he didn't want a lunatic to ruin the moment.

Picking up non-verbal communication wasn't one of Marlow's strong points. Body language was as foreign to her as French was. Coupled with her complete disregard for authority, something she had fostered in retaliation against her father, she failed to pick up the Officer's growing hostility and her next gasp of breath came out dripping with sarcasm.

"Well, I am impressed the finest law enforcement officers are trained to know the exact height of every kid in the country, yet are still unable to provide me with an answer to my question - was there a child onboard?"

The Officer had had enough. He took a step forward in what he hoped was a threatening manner, although he was a little alarmed that the woman held her ground. He raised the radio mic clipped to his fluorescent high-visibility jacket, in a warning that said '*I click this mic and you're gonna be nicked.*'

"If you don't get off the motorway immediately, I will arrest you for disturbing the peace."

"Disturbing the peace? This is a major accident. I'd say the peace has already been disturb-"

"AND," continued the Officer talking over her, "I can inform you that there was no child, baby, OAP, man, woman, or pet - other than the driver - aboard when we arrived."

Marlow threw her hands to the heavens. "Finally!" she

yelled. She shared a grin with the Officer. "Just one more thing, mate." She jerked a thumb in the direction the lorry was heading. "There's a service station a couple of miles from here, isn't there?"

DAN'S HANDS were still shaking as he gulped the lukewarm coffee. The taste allowed him to focus on the issue of why service station coffee was always sold so cold you had to drink it in several gulps or throw it away? He'd tried ice coffee once before and hadn't liked the taste, so tepid was hardly an improvement. Then again, he didn't really like the taste of coffee any more than the vile energy drinks he was forced to consume.

Diversion over, his mind leapt back to the moment he jolted awake in the lorry cab and straight into a waking nightmare just as it struck the central barrier. The Driver had screamed at the top of his lungs as their world jolted sideways. Dan felt his stomach lurch and was convinced if he'd eaten anything more substantial than a Mars bar, then they would also have had flying vomit to contend with as the lorry tipped over. The seatbelt kept him firmly in place, which was a good thing as his backpack was already airborne and struck the Driver in the face - silencing his terrified scream.

Out of the corner of his eye, Dan could see the road fill up the side window next to him. The wing mirror snapped off seconds before the lorry floundered and the side window smashed into a myriad of white safety glass shards aimed at his face. Sparks licked from the door as it scraped across the road. All around him it sounded as if the world was coming to an end.

Then it abruptly stopped.

They were no longer sliding. Metal was no longer eating

asphalt, and the engine was no longer screaming in overdrive. Dan was lodged sideways in his seat, the Driver unconscious above him, held in place by his belt. There was the distinct smell of diesel. Dan's head was spinning, both from the crash and the fumes. Even when he closed his eyes he could still feel the world wallowing sleepily around him. What had happened? Had they tried to avoid something in the road? Had there been a reckless driver ahead? His Grandpa had always told his mum that the most dangerous thing on the road were other drivers.

Or had it been another nightmare?

Dan shivered at the thought. How long had he been asleep? Minutes? Hours? How far had they travelled before the shades of his mind oozed into reality? With his sense of balance reeling, his mind churning and his nostrils filled with the increasingly acrid scent of fuel, Dan decided they should get out.

"Are you OK?" he said, reaching a trembling hand for the Driver. He didn't move. Dan gave him two sharp shakes, but still the man was unresponsive. For a horrible moment Dan thought the man was dead until he noticed the shallow rise of his chest.

"I'll get us out of here."

He unclipped his seatbelt and fell unceremoniously onto his backside, scrapping the tarmac through the shattered passenger window. He stood, bringing him level to the Driver's face. The man's nose was broken from impact with Dan's flying backpack. Bloodied bubbles formed on his lips as he breathed.

"Wake up," said Dan, shaking him. It was a lame thing to say, but he couldn't think of anything else. He'd watched enough terrible hospital dramas on TV that he should know what to do. He thought back - usually when somebody was lying bleeding on the floor the doctors... well, the doctors and nurses talked about who was sleeping with who and why.

Thinking about it, none of the TV shows he saw bore any resemblance to what people would really say. No wonder his Mum always insisted television wasn't educational.

"I'll get you out," he said, hoping that the Driver could hear him at some level. Dan thumbed the release switch on the Driver's seat belt–

And the Driver dropped towards him. Dan tried to catch him, but the man was far too heavy. He butted Dan in the chest and they crashed awkwardly to the floor where Dan had been sitting moments earlier.

"Crap." The man's weight crushed Dan. He had to use his feet to lever the bulky carcass off him. It was a good thing the Driver was still out cold. "Sorry about that."

The windscreen had shattered, but the safety glass had held together so it was now opaque and covered in a network of white lines like a spider's web. Dan experimentally touched it. It wobbled like plastic. He gave it two sharp kicks and the whole window crumpled onto the road beyond. Outside, he could now see a wall of traffic - the cars approaching from the opposite carriageway had halted seconds away from impact. Dan gripped the Driver under the armpits and pulled him a few feet across the road before he fell flat. The Driver's legs were still in the cab, caught on his seatbelt.

"Help me!" yelled Dan to anybody who might have been watching.

He pulled again, inching the Driver further out but hampered by both the belt and the Driver's mass. He heaved once more and was surprised when the Driver moved a few feet. Dan realised this was achieved because two drivers - one woman and a suited man - were helping him.

The woman was a picture of concern. "Are you alright?"

"I'm fine, but he's unconscious," said Dan.

Between the three of them, the Driver was easier to move

away from the danger zone. Dan became aware traffic on the motorway had ground to a halt, with many cars facing completely the wrong direction. People were wandering around – some injured and bleeding, others with mobile phones cradled against their ears. He caught snatches of conversation.

"Police... traffic accident... smell petrol..."

They dragged the Driver to the grassy bank and laid him down. The suited man took off his jacket and rolled up his sleeves.

"I'm a qualified first aider," he stated with some authority. "Roll him into the recovery position."

Dan and the woman had no idea what this was, so followed the suit's instructions to roll the Driver on his side and check he wasn't choking on his tongue. The man then began his inspection of the Driver as more people crowded around.

"An ambulance is on the way," somebody said.

"Stinks of fuel," said another, "It could blow up any second."

Dan suddenly realised his backpack was still in the cab. It contained all the possessions he now had in the world and didn't want to lose them. He darted back to retrieve it.

"You boy! No! It's too dangerous!" somebody shouted, but nobody tried to stop him.

With his backpack in hand, Dan finally saw the full trail of devastation behind them. His eyes drew to the trailer and the huge tears along the metal. There was no doubt in his mind what had caused the crash.

Swinging his backpack on, Dan sprinted across the far side of the carriageway – away from the Driver. He scrambled through the bushes on the inclined embankment, desperate to get far away. He heard voices call behind him, but he ignored them all. The greater the distance, the less harm he could inflict on others...

DAN PLACED his empty coffee cup down. The caffeine, combined with the adrenaline still flowing through him, would hopefully keep him awake for a couple more hours. He'd eventually have to find somewhere to sleep. Somewhere away from anybody he could harm. A vault in the middle of nowhere would be ideal.

It had taken him three hours to reach the service station, and the winter's night was already closing in. Worse, Dan noticed it was snowing, which meant sleeping in the open was now out of the question.

His stomach rumbled. He needed more than chocolate and crisps to keep him going. Luckily, the service station had a restaurant serving hot stodgy food that would help keep him awake. He left the café, ambling towards the restaurant as he counted the money in his pocket. Twelve pounds and some change was all he had. How was he supposed to get far with just that?

Contemplating how to make the cash last, he didn't notice a figure entering the service station until the very last second. The woman's long wavy wet hair was plastered against her forehead, but there was no mistaking the raggedy appearance of Marlow.

CHAPTER SEVEN

DAN BOLTED LIKE A JACKRABBIT. Marlow swore under her breath and gave chase as discretely as possible, although she was more than aware of the eyes following her as she pushed her way through a knot of people.

"Excuse me," she grunted.

She caught the word 'gypsy' muttered under a few of people's breaths. Ordinarily, when in a foul mood, she would round on such idiots and vent a piece of her mind, but now her eyes were fixed squarely on the boy as he fled into a shop.

Dan tried to duck between shelves, but Marlow had the height advantage and tracked the boy's bobbing head. The aisles were maze-like, but a few quick turns and Marlow had Dan cornered against a wall of magazines. The boy froze, his eyes darting to an old woman blocking his only escape route past the paperback section.

"Dan, it's me. You remember who I am?"

Dan scowled. "I know who you are. Keep away from me." He kept his voice low. If he drew attention to himself then security would surely come along and grab Marlow, but then he would have to answer several awkward questions too.

"Your Grandpa sent me to bring you back."

"I don't care. I'm not going back home!"

Marlow glanced around; everybody in the shop was staring at him. The sight of such a woman menacing a child was more than enough to have the place swarming with police.

"I'm his aunty," she said, forcing a grin. "Ain't that right, Dan?" She glared at Dan, defying him not to play along.

Dan looked up at the faces fixed expectantly on him. Now was the perfect chance to get Marlow off his case... and to end up with a caring Police Officer intent on reuniting him with his mother.

Dan gulped and forced a smile. "Sorry, Aunt. I just..."

"He had one of his turns. He's a little mental." Marlow ignored Dan's scowl. That seemed to get a collective nod of understanding and, as one, everybody turned away as if staring was the unkind thing to do. Marlow extended her hand to Dan and spoke a little louder than necessary. "What's say we sit down and get a drink, eh? Maybe some food. Calm down and talk things through."

Dan ignored the out-stretched grubby hand but nodded and followed Marlow from the shop. Marlow tried not to glower when the same people who had been cursing her under their breaths now whispered *poor woman* and other such platitudes to ease their own conscience as they passed.

Making sure Dan was always within arm's reach in case he bolted, Marlow led them to a café and ordered two mugs of coffee and the greasiest burger and fries they had. They sat near the window overlooking the motorway. It was now getting dark and snowing heavy; fat flakes clung to the glass, distorting the traffic below which had flowed once again, evidence that the lorry had finally been cleared.

"I heard the lorry driver'll live," grunted Marlow as she nibbled the food. "Lucky thing you didn't kill him." She took some satisfaction watching Dan squirm.

Dan wolfed the hot food, talking as he chewed. "It wasn't on purpose. Besides, I'd rather it was him than Mum or Gramps..." He took a gulp of coffee, refusing to meet Marlow's gaze, no doubt expecting to be berated for such a reckless regard for other people. Instead, he was surprised when he heard Marlow grunt in agreement.

"You know, when I was your age, I would've been happy if an Infiltrator had taken out my old man."

Dan flinched at the thought. "Why d'you call them Infiltrators? They're monsters. And when I was my age, I wished my dad could be here to help me." He whispered the last in a low sorrowful voice that made Marlow instantly regret her flippant comment.

"Nightmares infiltrate our world, raiding it like thieves in the night... day in your case." A long pause followed and Marlow felt compelled to add, "And I'm sure your dad was a much better bloke than mine."

That brought a fleeting smile to Dan's face, which was almost instantly shadowed by grief. "I don't know. I never met him."

Another silence. Marlow had no idea how to talk to kids. She had no idea how to talk to adults either, so decided that she might as well plough on.

"Look kid–"

"Dan. Not Daniel and definitely not 'kid'"

"Dan... look, your Grandpa and Mum're worried. You shouldn't have run away from home. What d'you expect it would achieve?"

"I expect the monsters won't kill them."

Marlow wasn't used to such a direct answer, she felt

awkward talking to children. "Well... there is that, but it's unlikely though. Your Infiltrators haven't attacked them yet, so there is no reason they would start now, right? Doesn't make much sense to feed so close to home." She instantly regretted the last comment when Dan looked at her with wide, frightened eyes.

"So they would!"

"Well, um, y'see... look, it ain't that simple..."

"The nightmares are getting worse, aren't they?" Marlow opened her mouth to answer, but Dan pressed on. "I never used to have them in the day, and at night they occasionally toppled furniture. Maybe smashed a mirror or scraped wallpaper." Dan snorted humourlessly. "And to think I used to believe it was me sleepwalking. What an idiot." He paused, then looked wistful. "I don't dream of them though. I never have nightmares. My dreams are always good... vivid. Sometimes I even realise I'm dreaming and can start controlling things. I can do whatever I want." He stared at Marlow as if expecting her to challenge the statement. Instead, Marlow shrugged.

"It's called lucid dreaming." She was not sure if she should try to console the boy or not. In fact, she had no idea what to say - which was probably part of the reason her own children didn't seem to miss her. She was never there with motherly advice or encouragement. The horrible truth was that Trebor had done a wonderful job in bringing them up. Something her own dad hadn't managed.

Marlow drifted back into the conversation when she realised that Dan had continued talking. "So we're agreed that going back is the wrong thing to do."

"Huh? I didn't say that."

"You implied it. Go back and my nightmares, Infiltrators, whatever, will kill them."

Marlow suspected Dan was good at manipulating people,

whether or not conscious of it. She suspected that the kid would grow up to be a lawyer. "Not necessarily..."

"They almost got the trucker who picked me up."

Marlow nodded. "Yeah, that was a dumb idea. What were you thinking?"

"I was thinking I better get far away, actually. You know, for an adult you're kind of weird."

Marlow instinctively spat back, the words slipping out before she could stop them. "And for a kid, you're a freak."

Dan glared at her. Marlow avoided his gaze and stared through the window as the snow gathered pace.

"Adults don't talk like that," said Dan. It was a mixture of accusation and uncertainty.

Marlow sensed Dan was used to getting his own way, probably mollycoddled by his worrying mother. "My job is to hunt these Nightmares and stop them from polluting our world. Not to babysit."

"You're not very good at either."

Marlow's hand shook as she controlled her temper, so much so that the coffee plopped over the rim of the cup as she slammed it down.

"I'm the bloody best, you little shit." Dan's eyes grew larger when Marlow swore. "And, quite frankly, you're the only real problem I ever had. See most *normal* kids," Marlow said the word slowly just to annoy him, "would have a single Infiltrator. A lone Nightmare that would work long and hard on the other side to open the portal as they slept. You are not supposed to channel more than one through. It's supposed to be impossible."

"Which makes me unique," said Dan with the ghost of a smile.

"That's certainly one word for it. If my old man could see you, it would have puzzled him - and he hated puzzles."

"I thought dreams were the subconscious playing out ideas and fantasies? At least that's what Doctor Donohue told me."

"I guess the good Doc doesn't know everything. I suppose some dreams are like that. You're able to act out amazing things, see incredible places..." her tone was tinged with longing. She noticed Dan's questioning frown, so cleared her throat and continued more authoritatively. "Whereas Conduits, that fre... folks like you, create a channel from their world into ours."

"But if dreams are all in the mind... how can these monsters, these Infiltrators, be real?"

"Oh, they come from a real place. Beyond your dreams, beyond what we can see around us. Innerspace. It's a very real world. I suppose scientists like to call such things parallel dimensions." Marlow shuddered at the thought of it. She had never crossed into the Nightmare realm, as far as she knew, nobody could, but she had glimpsed it through portals. A land of darkness and shadow where the Nightmares craved the warmth of our world. As a child, her father had forced her to stare into the void - and it had gazed back, full of fangs, claws and blood. It was a place no kid should ever be exposed to, yet that was her childhood. For a few seconds it irritated her to feel a jolt of sympathy towards Dan - before his grating voice cut in.

"Another dimension? Beyond sight and sound," he quoted from a television show he had caught one night.

"Exactly. Normally they would leave us alone, but some freeeee..." she bit off the word *freak*, "...are able to tap into their world. It takes the Infiltrators a long time. Months sometimes, to coax the Conduit to open enough for them to pass through. Then, as long as the Conduit remains asleep, they can roam free and rampage unchecked in our world. They never harm their Conduit, though. They're their only way in or out,

in fact they are very protective of that person. Once the Infiltrator has been eradicated here, the Conduit closes and, unless
another Nightmare takes great pains in opening the channel
again, that's it. That's why there are few Nightmares stalking
down your average city street at night."

Dan was thoughtful. "But my Nightmares keep coming.
Once you kill one another takes its place."

Marlow nodded. "My first thought was that it was
connected to your narcolepsy. That's an ideal affliction for the
Infiltrators, but after seeing the bad boys that keep coming
through, I think it's something else entirely. I just don't know
what."

Dan stared out of the window. The snow was sticking,
slowing traffic to a crawl.

"Like a motorway," he mused.

"Mmm? What?"

"If normal dreamers, Conduits, are like roads that can only
be used once, I'm more like a motorway. The Nightmares can
zoom through."

Marlow nodded. "Makes sense, I suppose."

"Does that means that bigger things can come through
too." Marlow's brow furrowed. "You can't get a lorry down a
country road, right?"

"That's an... interesting way of looking at it," Marlow
conceded.

A heavy silence passed between them as Dan finished the
rest of his food. Despite the initial buzz he experienced, he
could feel his energy was already flagging. After the lorry incident he was determined to find a way to control his narcolepsy.
At the moment a single thought kept him awake.

"Which makes me wonder how big they're going to get."

Marlow shuffled in her seat. The same thought was
bugging her too. She pushed her cups aside. She was beginning

to feel jittery, and in her line of work that was not a good thing.

"Come on, ki... Dan. Time to get you home." She started to rise, but saw that he made no motions to leave.

"Are you kidding? After everything you just told me? Or maybe you didn't understand exactly what 'running away from home' actually means?"

Marlow slumped back in the chair. "Come on! I thought we had a rapport going on here. That we understood one another?"

"Then you thought wrong, big style."

Marlow thumped both palms on the table in irritation. "I *need* to get you home. Your Grandpa's paying me to haul your butt back in one piece."

"I don't care! I'm *never* going back!" he glared at Marlow. His steely gaze made Marlow look away. "Not until these nightmares stop."

"They might never..." Marlow began, but stopped when she saw the fear in the kid's eyes.

Dan gripped the edge of the table with both hands, partly determined not to move, but mostly to stop himself falling face-first asleep into the table. "I'm not going back until these Nightmares stop. That's the deal. You're supposed to be the expert, and Gramps is paying you to make them stop - so do your job!"

Marlow stood up, impulsively contemplating walking out. The brat's impetuous tone was annoying and, for a fleeting second, he reminded her of her father. In a flash Marlow thought all things she wanted to say aloud:

Fine, run away and get your dumb-self killed, see if I care! I don't need your Grandpa's stupid money and I don't need your hassle!

The problem was, she needed the cash, but that wasn't the whole reason she'd bit her tongue. As much as she resented the family business - and she despised with a passion the fact she'd inherited it with little thought from her father about what *she* would rather to do with her life - she was intrigued. No Nightmare had bested her before, and she wasn't about to let one do it now. Then, left unchecked, there was the wake of destruction that Dan had already left behind. How many more lives would the creatures destroy? And, as much as it loathed her, she felt a modicum of responsibility. While she couldn't imagine the dreams the boy experience, and that was something that stoked jealousy, they had a common middle ground with the Infiltrators.

Marlow slumped back down and truculently folded her arms. "So what now? Like I said, I'm not babysitting you for the rest of your life, *kid*." She had hoped to elicit a reaction from Dan, but the boy was above such juvenile mind games. He looked thoughtful, and more than a little tired.

"Help me," Dan finally said in a low voice. "Whatever it takes. I can't let my family get hurt. They're all I've got."

His voice was low and pathetic. Marlow wondered if her own children would respond with such passion at the thought of never seeing their mother again. Then again, they'd already forgotten her, and guessed that Trebor had probably already invented a convincing story to explain her long absence away.

For the second time that day, Marlow experienced her emotions trump reason as she spoke on autopilot. "OK then. Let's see what we can do." Dan smiled, and Marlow wondered if it was a genuine smile of relief or the victorious smile of manipulation.

Marlow *really* didn't like the kid.

CHAPTER EIGHT

THEY CHECKED into the Travel Stop hotel attached to the service station. Dan had been drifting dangerously close to sleep and assured her that no amount of coffee would keep him awake. He was probably O.D.ing on the stuff right now, and his body was rebelling.

Marlow bought a dozen energy drinks to keep herself and Dan awake and dug her dirty fingernails into Dan's arm, focusing on a pressure point that delivered just enough pain to keep him awake for the walk across the car park.

Marlow rented a room for her and her 'nephew' using money she could ill-afford to spend, and should really go towards her son's birthday, which she'd momentarily forgotten about. Once again, she had promised to send Trebor money. How could such a simple thing slip her mind? As usual she blamed such lapses on her condition. The lack of quality sleep must be ruining her short-term memory. Or was that just an excuse to hide her absent-mindedness? Marlow stopped slapping her forehead at the reception desk when the receptionist gave her a quizzical look.

The room was an exact duplicate to the one Dan had stayed in the night before, right down to the painting of abstract lollypop trees opposite the bed.

"I need to get my gear out of the car," Marlow said. "You going to be OK for a few minutes?"

Dan sat on the end of the bed, the television remote already in his hand. "Sure." The television blinked alive and Dan cranked the volume of a comedy show that was playing. He nodded reassuringly at Marlow. "I'll be fine for another thirty minutes or so."

Marlow darted outside where the snow was now being driven by a gale, caught in the car park's floodlights. Despite the storm, the service station was still quite busy. Marlow wished that wasn't the case, the more people around the more danger they were in if one of Dan's 'mares got loose, but the weather was encouraging people to pull over and take a break and there was nothing she could do about that.

The cold was already piercing her trench coat by the time she reached the Beetle. Freezing fingers fumbled through the keys as she unlocked the door and sat inside for protection from the elements. It was too dark to see anything, and her interior light had died long ago, so she groped around the backseat, searching for the kit bag. She fingered the straps and hauled it onto the passenger seat to quickly checked the contents: her short barrelled blunderbuss, several boxes of cartridges, a baseball bat, a high-beam LED torch and a few other items a savvy nightmare hunter always kept to hand.

She was about to climb out when she noticed Dan's mobile phone had slipped down the side of her seat. She had forgotten about it. Thumbing the button, the cracked screen illuminated, a message showed that it was now fully charged. She considered ringing Trebor to stem the tide of abuse he would surely throw at her for not sending money as promised. It was now snowing so ferociously it blotted the windscreen. The view beyond resembled an abstract painting. Jamie's birthday was still four days away... she was pretty sure of that. She could send the money tomorrow. Hell, she might even turn up with it in person...

Or was it was tomorrow? What kind of parent would forget a detail like that - except her own dad, of course.

She pocketed the phone and decided to sort it out tomorrow after she'd slept on it. She glanced back up - and suddenly flinched in fear. The muzzle of a large black dog pressed against the windshield. At first she thought it was a trick of the light through the thin layer of snow across the windscreen. Then the vehicle rocked as the enormous beast shifted position on the bonnet. *Nightmarus Canineus* - she had faced one before. Once was enough never to forget.

Marlow pressed back in the seat, desperately trying to focus on the shifting image as the snow obscured it; her left hand slowly reaching for the gun and her fingers ran down the stock, but as she lifted it the funnelled barrel caught in the handles of the bag. Her eyes flicked to the problem, and she deftly twisted the weapon free – only to look back out of the window to see that the beast had gone.

With her heart pounding, Marlow leapt from the vehicle, quickly scanning the car park. There were no footprints, but there were a million shadows in which the creature could lurk. She raised the gun with hands that trembled partly from nerves, but mostly from the cold. Across the car park a couple ran to their car, the man gallantly shielding the girl's head with his own coat. There was no sign of the beast.

Marlow circled her car. There was a foot of clearance between the Beetle's chassis and the ground: plenty of space for an Infiltrator to hide. She knelt, her kneecaps cricking painfully. She couldn't see fully underneath so, holding the blunderbuss out lest anything pounced, she dropped to her knees and propped herself up with one hand, then peered under the car.

Nothing.

With more effort than she would have liked, Marlow climbed back to her feet. She completed her path around the vehicle but saw no sign of anything unusual. Had it gone? Impossible, surely a nightmare would fight to protect its Conduit - and there was no bigger threat than Marlow. Then where was it? Or had she dreamt it?

Impossible, of course. She let the idea slide. She couldn't have dreamt it if she tried, which meant it had to be real.

And that meant Dan was asleep.

"Shit!" Marlow grabbed her kit bag from the car, shoving the blunderbuss inside. She sprinted across the car park, snow seeping into her boots, making her feet uncomfortably wet.

There was nobody at the reception desk as Marlow barrelled through. With a sense of dread, she wondered if that was a bad sign. Fighting for breath, she pounded up the stairs two at a time and sprinted down the corridor, past identical doorways, through two sets of fire doors that bore smiling faces with drooping eyes and night cap perched jauntily to the side, a speech bubble read '*Sssh, guests are sleeping!*'

Marlow fervently hoped that was not the case.

She reached the room and tried the electronic key card in the lock. A red light flashed and the door remained resolutely closed.

"What the hell?" She tried again. She could hear the television inside. Once more the red light flashed. She was about to hammer on the door, not that it would wake somebody like Dan - and would certainly sound like a dinner bell ringing to any beast lurking within - when she realised that she'd inserted it the wrong way round. She swiped it again. This time the light beeped green. Marlow dropped the kit bag - her hand squeezing the blunderbuss's stock as it fell away - and shouldered the door open.

Dan was exactly where Marlow had left him, staring at the screen. He jumped as Marlow ran in and his face paled at the sight of the gun pointing at him.

"What did I do?" Dan spluttered.

Marlow combed the gun across the ceiling, eyes scanning around the room in confusion.

"You're awake!"

"Told you," Dan held up a half empty energy drink then nodded towards the television. "I've never seen this show before. It's quite funny."

"But I saw... I thought I saw..."

Marlow propped the blunderbuss against the table, used her foot to drag the bag into the room, and closed the door.

"What?"

Marlow thought for a moment. What had she seen? A trick of the light? No, the car had moved... hadn't it? She'd been a Hunter all her life. Disciplined training had forced her to see what was really in the corner of her eye, or define the vaguest shape in the darkness. It was a matter of life and death to be able to spot the things most people either missed or had to look twice to see.

"I thought I saw an Infiltrator out in the car park."

Dan's eyes went wide. "I was awake, I swear. Ask me anything about the show." He pointed at the TV.

Marlow recalled Dan's expression as she'd run inside. His eyes were open, his head upright. It was not the slouched repose of somebody caught slumbering. Besides, the kid had no reason to lie. The whole reason they were here was to deal with the problem, not avoid it.

Dan turned the TV off. "Could it have been... somebody else's?"

Once again, Marlow saw on his face a look of genuine fear. It brought back a memory of what she had seen so many times in the mirror when she had been that age. For the first time Marlow understood how terrified Dan was. The video he'd watched of the Infiltration at home was enough to scare him into running away from his family for ever. This wasn't a kid who thought it was all some stupid joke played by adults or a superpower they could wield at night - as many of the brats did. No, this was somebody frightened, not just for their own life, but for those he cared about. Somebody who had witnessed the destruction a bad dream could leave.

Marlow forced a smile. "Nah, impossible. Conduits are never clustered together like that. You might get one or two in the same town at the same time, but that's a *very* rare event."

"As rare as having repeat episodes? As rare as a daymare?" Dan's voice broke as he spoke.

The same thought had crossed Marlow's mind, but now was not the time to speculate. What he needed was a little parental reassurance - something Marlow was useless at dispensing. Instead, she turned her back to Dan so the boy couldn't see her doubt and began emptying the kit bag.

"Don't worry about it. I was mistaken, is all. I'm tired. Here," she threw his mobile to him. "You'd left it in the other hotel."

Dan hesitated for a moment, then checked it was on airplane mode before tucking it into his jacket pocket. "Maybe you fell asleep and dreamt there was another monster outside?" He was being playful, but Marlow's cold realism trampled it.

"No chance. I don't dream."

She pulled out a set of three small tripod-mounted lights and positioned them around the bed. Behind each bulb a silver reflector fanned out to amplify the light. She caught Dan's curious expression.

"High-lux beams. Powerful ultra-violet lamps." She plugged one in and flicked a switch at the back of the lamp. A powerful white-light issued out, brighter than Dan thought was possible for such a tiny light. He shielded his eyes as Marlow angled the light so it played around the bed, vanquishing shadows. "They travel through the shadows so this gives the buggers less room to hide," she explained, thankful that the hotel divan had only an inch clearance from the floor. Still, an inch of darkness was an infinite ocean for an Infiltrator.

"Everybody dreams," Dan said dismissively as Marlow set the next light up.

"Not me."

More light flooded the room on the opposite side of the bed, illuminating under the desk and highlighting the colours of the room.

Dan squinted as his eyes slowly adjusted. "That's just something people say because they don't remember, but everybody dreams all the time. An average of six dreams every night in fact."

The first two lights were positioned low and sent stark shadows across the ceiling, so Marlow angled the third light upwards to dispense them. "Like I said, I don't dream. It's a clinical thing. Never have been able to. That part of me brain just don't seem to work right."

Dan was shocked. "Like *ever*?"

"Like ever," Marlow confirmed, activating the last light to sweeping the ceiling shadows away.

"That's terrible. I've always dreamt about things. Cool

things like having superpowers. Once I had a really vivid one that I was in space piloting a star fighter. It was so realistic, I seemed to know everybody around me, but then I realised it was a dream. Do you know the moment that happens you can take control and do whatever you want. You said it was called lucid dreaming? They're the best. You've suddenly got the power to create things, be anybody, see anyone you want to..." He drifted off thoughtfully and after a moment's silence he added: "I couldn't imagine never having a dream."

Marlow sat the blunderbuss cartridges upright on the table and made sure she had several spares in her pockets. She looked quizzically at Dan. "Ain't you tired yet?"

Dan shook his head. He looked more awake than Marlow had ever seen him.

"So why can't you dream?" Marlow shrugged and propped the baseball bat near the door. The bat's surface was chipped and dented from the many uses it had served outside of sports. "You must have done as a kid, surely?"

Marlow sighed. "As far as I'm concerned, I had the dreams frightened outta my skull by my old man." She pulled a pair of night vision goggles from the bag and hung them around her neck.

"Why? What did he do?" Dan crawled under the bed sheets, still fully dressed. He only paused to kick his trainers off.

Marlow pulled the kit bag to her side, it still had a few other tools she could use to fight with if things got desperate. Satisfied, she pulled the chair from under the room's desk and angled it between the bed and the window, keeping as far as she could from Dan to maximise her reaction time when the Infiltrator came. With a weary sigh, she sat down and rested the blunderbuss across her knees.

"When I was your age, he'd drag me out on hunts like this."

"Wow. That sounds so cool! If you're not the one doing the Conduiting, that is."

"It wasn't, believe me, it was bloody terrifying. I didn't want to know what he did. I didn't wanna think about it and I didn't want to do it myself, but he forced me. Said it would make the difference between life and death."

Memories flickered cross the dark screen of her mind. Her father's voice always encouraging as Marlow clutched a feeble weapon - a bat, a rusty sword, a plank with a nail in it - always poorly armed to face the malignant terrors. Claws, fangs, blazing blue eyes or hollow black ones peered back at her while her father excitedly reeled off what was about to consume her whole.

Serpentinius Dreamtus.

Vulgaris Nightum.

Mortis Morphosum.

Marlow could recall them all by rote. Her father would fearlessly yell their names at each encounter. Nothing frightened him.

Nothing.

Except one word that was occasionally uttered between her father and her grandpa: *Darkmare*. When pressed to what that meant, they would just shake their heads and mumble that some things in the Nightmare Realm were best left alone. If Marlow ever tried to press for more information her father would snap and order her to perform fifty press-ups or run a lap of the playing field - punishments designed so that Marlow was fit enough to maintain a *constant state of readiness*. Ready for whatever the world, or netherworld, might throw at her.

"I faced other people's bad dreams almost every single night. Maybe my brain shut down and refused to let me have any of my own. So, I have never been able to dream and you know what? It sucks to think about that. Sucks to think that everybody else can. All you gotta do is close your eyes and go to someplace else. You have no idea what an amazing gift that is."

"But look what you can do now," said Dan with genuine awe. "You can beat these things. You can stand up to them. That's something nobody else can do."

Marlow had often wondered if there were other Nightmare Hunters out there. Her father said it was a calling passed through generations, and the inability to dream came with it. Her grandpa had told tales of hunting teams that rode up and down the land, saving villages from the evils that prowled the dark. But never once had Marlow seen or heard of another Hunter these days. Maybe she was the last of her kind?

"You want to know something weird?" said Dan.

Marlow smiled. "If you can say something weirder than what we're doing, go for it."

"I've *never* had a nightmare. My dreams... they've always been kinda cool."

"That's Infiltrators for you. They administer a kind of anaesthetic to their Conduit. They don't want you waking up in the middle of the night and severing the portal." She indicated to the lamps. "Besides, they don't like UV light. That's why your daymares don't last too long. They make sure you have the most riotously enjoyable dreams to keep you slumbering."

Silence. For a second Marlow thought Dan was asleep, but instead he looked thoughtful.

"How do they deliver their anaesthetic?"

"As far as I can tell, it's a chemical they create inside the body, like a natural hormone."

"So if you could extract that... could you then take it?
Would it make you dream?"

Marlow was surprised by Dan's logic. That had never
occurred to her. "You know what... it just might. If we knew
what to look for and how to extract it, that is. My old man was
into that sort of thing. Always mixing chemicals and making
stupid herbal remedies."

Dan rolled onto his back and stared at the ceiling. His
mind was already racing with possibilities.

"That would be so cool. You know, you were lucky to have
a dad like that."

Marlow snorted derisively; she couldn't hold it back.
"Lucky? He destroyed my life. By the time I was fourteen, I
had no friends. Other kids were terrified of me. I'd seen so
many horrors that my hair turned white." Marlow gripped a
handful of damp black hair. "This comes outta a bottle."

Dan shrugged. "He showed you things nobody else has
seen. He taught you a skill nobody else has. I think that's
pretty amazing. I wish my dad had been around to teach me
something – anything – so I could do something nobody else
could."

Marlow stared at him, searching for traces of sarcasm. She
wanted to snap at how wrong he was. How having such an
overbearing father had turned her into a dreamless screwball
who was unable to even talk to her own kids, but something
struck a chord. Dan was painting Marlow's father in a new
light, one that was a stranger to Marlow.

"Maybe one day, when you have children, you could pass
your secrets on?" said Dan. His voice was now distinctly
slurred as he fought sleep.

"I've already got kids. Two of them. They hate me too."

Dan laughed, a short sharp bark. "*You* have children? Ha!
That's soooo funny."

Marlow shuffled in the seat, uncomfortable at being grilled by a thirteen-year-old.

"Why is that funny?"

Dan didn't reply. He was sound asleep; already his eyes darting in deep REM sleep behind closed lids. Marlow looked around the room, waiting for the first signs of attack.

It was a real shame... the kid was starting to get interesting.

CHAPTER NINE

SOMETHING WAS SERIOUSLY WRONG. Marlow had been a hunter for far too long and knew her enemies' proclivities. The moment a Conduit was asleep the bridge between worlds opened and the Infiltrators, eager for the warmth, energy and food from a rich new world, would slip through as swiftly as possible to make the most of it. So far Dan had been asleep for close to an hour and *nothing* had emerged.

Marlow hoped that the incident onboard the lorry had somehow been the last one. Had something happened then to sever Dan's link for ever? Could this be the end of his curse? Maybe the beast that had emerged had been killed when the lorry crashed?

No. It couldn't be that easy. It never was.

The spotlights held the shadows at bay, but even they didn't have the power to hold back a determined Infiltrator. Marlow's eyes slid from Dan, still lying in the same awkward slumbering position, to the only void of darkness left: the bathroom. The door was closed and Marlow berated herself for not switching on the light and leaving it ajar.

She strained to listen, but heard no signs of movement from within, and Nightmares were not known for their patience. Still, she slowly stood and crabbed toward the door, not once taking her eyes off Dan.

It was difficult to grip the spherical door handle while wielding a sawn-off blunderbuss. She heard the latch click and nudged the door ajar with her boot. The trio of powerful spotlights in the room did little to illuminate the Stygian blackness within the windowless bathroom.

Marlow flinched when a huge shadow loomed before her. Instinctively she raised the gun, finger pulling the trigger before she realised what she was looking at. Luckily, the gun's old trigger was in serious need of oiling and took a considerable amount of pressure to move, so her reflection was saved from being blown away.

She flicked the light switch and a feeble florescent tube erratically flickered a few of times before illuminating with an irritating hum as it filled the room with a cold blue-tinged light that beached all colour.

There was nothing in here.

Marlow was so on edge that she jumped when the television suddenly turned on, a political show blaring from the speakers. She ducked back into the room to see Dan was sitting upright in bed, wide awake and glued to the TV.

"You scared the crap outta me," she huffed as she sat back down. "Turn the volume down."

Dan didn't seem to hear, he was too absorbed with the show. Marlow frowned, she knew her ability to relate to the younger generation was poor, but she had no idea kids were so engaged by politics these days.

"C'mon, turn it down before somebody complains."

When Dan didn't act, Marlow found herself getting annoyed. She opened her mouth, ready to say something bitter

- when she noticed the TV remote control was at the bottom of the bed where Dan had tossed it. How had the kid turned it on?

A gentle icy tickle told her that something was amiss. Marlow slowly blocked the view between Dan and the TV. The boy didn't try to crane around her to continue watching, nor was there a word of protest, yet his eyes were still wide open and staring.

Marlow waved her hand in front of him, waiting for a reaction. She was rewarded with a short snorting from the kid.

Dan was still asleep.

A crashing wave of thoughts swam through Marlow's head. She'd studied somnology and oneirology, the sciences of sleep and dreams respectively - in fact her father had forced the theory-heavy subjects upon her. She knew some folks could sleep with their eyes open and, other than suffer from irritatingly dry eyes, still had a good night's sleep. It also explained what Marlow had seen in the car park. Dan had thought he'd been awake, but he must have experienced a micro-nap and only Marlow's arrival had awoken him. As his eyes were already wide open, he was convinced that he'd been awake the whole time.

The hairs on the back of Marlow's neck rose. She knew without a doubt that the Infiltrator was deliberately exploiting all of Dan's foibles. It didn't fit the regular pattern for one reason - it was setting a trap to catch the hunter.

The wave of trepidation that gripped Marlow's stomach now lurched into full-blown fear. Something more sinister than the average Nightmare was at work here. Before she could guess what that might be, the window imploded with such force that chunks of the wall's sheetrock around it splintered apart. Snow, broken glass and fragments of twisted window frame pelted Marlow as a coiling tentacle, as thick as a tractor's tyre, unfurled through the gap and plucked her out into the driving rain.

Marlow was hoisted out and above the building's roof. Snow stung her eyes, but she could see enough to notice the lights across the car park were extinguished. Her ribs felt ready to crack as the tentacle spun her around and she finally saw the fiend had spewed from the *other place*.

It was colossal. Sitting on the roof like a giant octopus. Midnight black skin made details almost impossible to see. She could make out at least four other tentacles draped across the roof slates and dangling down the side of the hotel to give it purchase. Another two slightly shorter limbs flailed, while a seventh brought Marlow closer to the Nightmare's vertical slit of a mouth. Despite the creature's size, the teeth were no longer than Marlow's hand, not that that comforted her as there were *thousands* of them tiered in several rows. Each leading further into the cavernous gullet. The fangs looked almost opaque, laced with crimson veins. As they gnashed together they created hellish sparks. Atop its head was a nest of coal-black eyes that had multiplied across its brow like acne. It let out a hideous roar – a mix between Godzilla and a car alarm.

It was the largest nightmare Marlow had ever seen, and there was certainly no name for it in her father's precious tome. It was new.

The cavernous mouth was feet away. Marlow felt the breath sucked out of her as the coils around her waist constricted. She attempted to breathe, but the little air she could draw in stank of the putrefying fish stench coming from the beast.

Luckily the tentacle had wrapped beneath her arms, leaving them free. Even more fortuitously, Marlow still had her gun. She was moving too fast and feeling too disoriented to take aim. Instead, wild reflexes honed from a lifetime of training kicked in, and Marlow shot at the beast's eyes.

The shriek the Infiltrator gave, as a cluster of eyeballs exploded like vile black grapes, drowned the gun's report. The tentacle around her waist slackened, and she fell–

Fortunately not far. She landed on roof tiles slick with fresh snow. Her arms windmilled for balance, the blunderbuss flipping from her grasp. It clattered along the tiles, then slid off the roof. The roof itself vibrated as the creature moved. Marlow's boots couldn't maintain their grip as she slipped inexorably towards the edge. Arms still crazily spinning, she slipped off the edge.

A fall from a single storey is enough to kill somebody. Marlow was saved from the three-storey plunge by landing in a fragile cherry blossom that was bare in the winter. The barren branches stabbed into her back before snapping and pitching her down and away from the building – straight onto the bonnet of a parked car. The metal buckled under her weight and the suspension bounced several times, triggering the alarm.

Marlow rolled from the vehicle and swayed unsteadily on her feet. Above, the nightmare was still very much there. It raised itself up on four thick tentacles and, using them as legs, it oozed over the side of the building and into the car park, crushing a dozen vehicles.

She looked around for the gun... it must be close, but it was too dark to see anything. The only light now came from the service station across the car park where four people had stopped to stare at the commotion. They obviously couldn't make anything out through the swirling snow because they were not yet fleeing in terror.

The nightmare roared again, flipping a van aside like an empty can. The vehicle bounced towards Marlow, forcing her to push herself flat in the snow as it spun narrowly overhead, colliding with the car she'd landed on.

Marlow scrambled for her life as the beast surged towards her. This was ridiculous! 'mares didn't get this big. Sure, she'd fought many the size of a van and once, even a coach. But this was *enormous*. Now the four gawkers got a clear look at the beast and decided to scream and run. Marlow needed a plan, fast.

Waking Dan would be futile; the Nightmare would have ensured his Conduit was sedated with enough pleasant dreams for that to happen. Her beloved blunderbuss was lost and useless against the titan. The traps she had brought along to ensnare the 'mare were likewise pathetic.

Another roar came close behind, and Marlow could feel the air displaced as tentacles swung for her. She switched directions, sprinting a sharp ninety degrees to her left just as the crash of broken cars and squeal of alarms behind rose to a crescendo. Marlow squinted as snow stung her eyes. She raised a hand to shield them as the glare from a lorry's headlights almost blinded her as it pulled into the service station.

Marlow had a sudden inspiration. She raced towards the lorry, heart hammering and every muscle in her legs protesting. She hated herself for drinking so much and eating so badly that her once trim frame had transformed into a pending cardiac attack. Marlow promised to whoever was listening that she'd quit drinking and get back in shape, if only she could survive the night.

Marlow protected her face with both forearms as she sprinted through a hedge separating the car park from the lorry park. A roar confirmed the beast was fifteen seconds behind and closing in.

The lorry swung towards Marlow as it lined up to a parking bay. The brakes suddenly slammed on. She didn't think the driver was trying to avoid her – he'd probably seen the monstrosity looming in his headlights.

Marlow reached the vehicle and grabbed the door handle, hoisting herself up the two steps that brought her level to the driver just as the man opened the door.

"I need your ride!" she yelled and pushed against the bewildered trucker. The man was bigger than her, with muscles bulging from his arms – but he obediently shuffled over to the passenger seat as Marlow swung in and crunched the lorry into gear. It crept forward. She had been hoping to run the terror over, but the lorry was accelerating at a snail's pace as it hauled the load behind it. She was already in third gear and moving at a brisk walking pace when the beast caught up and bumped undramatically against the vehicle. Tentacles wrapped around the cab as it hitched a ride. All Marlow and the trucker could see from within was an enormous mouth filling every inch of the windscreen and offering an unrivalled view down the monster's gullet.

"What is that?" the trucker wailed in an unseemly high-pitched voice.

"You ever had a bad dream?" Marlow grunted as she pushed into fourth gears and gained momentum. The lorry jerked as something struck the creature and a faint crunch of metal resonated just below the Nightmare's roar that plastered globs of spittle across the windscreen, forcing the Driver to reach over and put the wipers on out of habit.

"We've hit something!" he cried, not yet having got to grips with the reality of the situation.

"That's the idea!" snarled Marlow as she mashed the accelerator and crunched up another gear. Her internal radar hoped they were heading for the service station – and she prayed that people would see the lorry speeding towards them with the giant beast chewing open the cab. They felt three more jolts as she knocked vehicles aside but couldn't see anything. Marlow hammered the horn for added attention.

"Get ready to jump!" she warned.

The trucker looked at the door but made no move to get out.

"How?"

Marlow glanced at both side windows and spotted the flaw in her plan - huge tentacles lay across them, holding the creature in place and effectively sealing them inside.

"Oh, cr– "

The cab gave an enormous jolt, first pitching them forwards with such force Marlow headbutted the steering wheel - then they were both thrust back into their seats as the front of the cab rose almost forty degrees with an ear-splitting crash – before bouncing back to earth. They abruptly stopped moving forwards. The beast wailed before exploding, showering the windscreen in thick indigo goo.

Marlow felt dizzy and could already feel a bump forming on her forehead. She killed the engine and climbed from the cab, feet slipping in the deep-purple ichor oozing across on the tiled floor. All around she could hear screams and, as she got her bearings, she could now see they had rammed into the service station's atrium and skidded to a halt several yards inside, smashing into the magazine shop Marlow had cornered Dan in earlier.

Metal spars had given way under the impact and the remains of the glass roof that hadn't yet collapsed, groaned ominously. Only a few of the toughened glass panels had actually broken and everything was covered in rapidly evaporating nightmare gloop. Marlow was satisfied with her handiwork.

"Run! Everybody run!"

Marlow looked around, assuming that somebody had belatedly spotted the truck and attached monster, before realising that it was the trucker. Twisting further around, she saw water pouring over the floor from the lorry's load. It was a few more seconds before the fishy stench of the dead nightmare was replaced by sickening chemical fumes. Only then did it dawn on Marlow that she had commandeered a tanker.

"Oh crud," she muttered before turning around, waving her arms frantically and yelling : "Move! Go! Get outta here!" The fumes burned the back of her throat, sucked her warning into a hacking cough. Luckily nobody needed any motivation; they were already fleeing the disaster.

Marlow hopscotched over dry areas of the floor as she tried to avoid the liquid sloshing across the floor. A faint curtain of vapours rose as it melted the floor beneath. Marlow looked up to see fallen sections of roof blocked direct access to the exit and skirting around it took up extra valuable seconds.

Yards away was a broken window, jagged glass still hanging from the frame. She had little choice but to run towards it and jump through, protecting her head with both forearms. A jagged shard ripped the sleeve of her coat – then she landed in snowy slush outside, spilled and fell hard onto her side. But she was out – and that was all that was important.

She clambered on all-fours, intent on putting distance between her and the chemical spillage. Then she heard the unmistakable sounds of a child crying. At some primeval level it even got through to her blunt sense. She stopped - again wasting valuable seconds. It could easily be a trap set by another nightmare, but then she spotted a little girl cowering under a book display back in the shop. A steel roof spar had given way and collapsed through the store, forcing the girl to hide. Lighting fixtures had severed and now electrical cables dangled like snakes all around her, spitting spark.

"Mummy!" wailed the girl , tears cascading down her cheeks. She couldn't have been more than four.

Marlow tensed. Self-preservation screamed that she should run. But she sprinted back inside the building, skirting around the increasing pool of corrosive chemicals. She powered into the store, slipping on fallen books underfoot. A live cable glanced off her damp coat, but the live ends failed to make contact. Instead, they spat a warning spark near her face.

The little girl looked up at Marlow with wide eyes. Perhaps her unkept appearance was making the kid hesitate to accept salvation.

"Gimme your hand, darling," Marlow said in the sweetest voice she could muster. She risked a glance behind and quelled her rising panic as the tidal wave of liquid gushed into the shop. She turned back to the girl, her eyes staring madly as her false grin broadened. A look that made the child actually back away.

"Don't be as dumb as you look," Marlow said with a smile. "Take my hand."

The girl hesitated - only springing forward to take the filthy hand as half the shop collapsed down behind her with a deafening sound of masonry. Marlow lifted the child up, hooked an arm to cradle the girl as she turned and ran.

Even avoiding the pooling liquid, her feet slipped on the wet floor as snow blew inside. She focused on the opening to the car park ahead, the intact automatic door constantly opening and closing with an asthmatic hiss. The kid's grip tightened as more roof collapsed behind. Marlow couldn't see, but judging by the noise and the girl's gasp, she guessed a sparking cable had ignited the liquid payload.

There was a loud WHUMP from behind. Marlow dared not turn as the wind rushed past her with hurricane force - feeding the flames. Then she was through the door just as it sliced closed behind her. A moment later she felt a wall of heat singe her back as a massive explosion blossomed within the shopping area and the ground ahead lit up as if the sun had crashed the party.

Glass from the door pelted her back. The snow's chill helped lessen some of the heat blast from the explosion. Marlow didn't look back. She kept running towards the shadows, vaguely aware that the fleeing service station punters had congregated there.

Another explosion came. It was a brief boom - at least for those standing close as they became temporarily deaf. A pressure wave thrust Marlow to the snowy grass, still clutching the girl. She instinctively twisted herself over the kid to take the brunt of the impact. An orange mushroom cloud punched into the night sky, illuminating the car park. Debris were tossed vertically up like matchsticks, and the severed halves of the tanker somersaulted straight up before crashing back into the inferno.

Shaking, Marlow sat up. The girl had stopped crying and stared at the inferno, no doubt the coolest thing she had ever seen.

"India!" gasped a voice next to Marlow, and the girl tugged from her arms by her tearful mother. They both embraced in tears, their elation left no time to thank Marlow.

"You're welcome," she muttered, suddenly remembering what she disliked about other people, namely: everything. Then she remembered the cause of the debacle. "Dan!"

THE EXPLOSION HAD JOLTED Dan awake now that the Infiltrator's sedative was no longer active. Still, the noise had only registered in the back of his consciousness. He'd rolled over as every window in the Travel Stop imploded, pelting his duvet with glass. That was more than enough to wake him.

When Marlow entered at a run, Dan had been staring

through the broken window at the farrago outside, watching the crowds keep their distance from the service station wreckage, huddling together as the snow eased.

"We're leaving!" The exploding windows had taken out two of the lights, but Marlow shoved everything haphazardly into her kit bag. "Right now."

Outside, Marlow felt nothing but amazement to see her Beetle was one of the few cars the monster hadn't crushed. Just as fortuitous, she found her blunderbuss under a lamppost that had come back to life now the fiend's portal was closed.

The Volkswagen started on the fourth attempt and they sped onto the motorway just as flickering blue lights behind announced the late arrival of the emergency services.

"Where are we going?" asked Dan.

"Far from here," although in truth Marlow had no idea what to do. She was not only out of her league, but in a completely different sport.

CHAPTER TEN

"You know what your problem is?"

Marlow vaguely harrumphed for Dan to continue as she concentrated on driving through the snow. Not that she was really paying attention, but as long as the kid was prattling away, then at least he wasn't sleeping. They had stopped twice to buy coffee, energy drinks, chocolate bars and fuel. She mused that Dan's blood sugar was probably so high that a normal person wouldn't be able to sleep for a day, although the kid showed no outward effects.

"Well, it's not like it's a *single* problem, really. More lots of different ones percolating to make... well, you, really," said Dan thoughtfully.

The honesty of children, thought Marlow. Another reason she disliked them.

"For starters, you said you have children? How old are they? Eighteen? Older?"

"None of your business," she muttered, trying to concentrate on the road.

"And I bet they left home as soon as they could rather than hang around with you."

"Just how old do you think I am?" She shot him a glance - wobbling the car across the road. She gripped the wheel and concentrated. She was feeling exhausted but wanted to put as much distance between them and the incident as possible. Keeping away from the motorway, she'd found the A-roads were almost deserted in the wee hours of the night. "If you really want to know, they're about your age actually and, unlike you, they haven't run away from home." The comment came out rather more sharply than Marlow had intended.

"You mean they're not freaks?" said Dan in a low voice. He stared straight ahead, and Marlow hoped he hadn't fallen asleep with his eyes open again.

"I didn't mean..."

"It's OK. I'm used to it. You're no different from the morons in school." The calm, matter-of-fact manner in which he spoke sounded more mature than Marlow's own monosyllabic responses. Not for the first time she felt that she wasn't the grown up in this conversation.

"They live with their father."

"So you're divorced? Makes sense."

Marlow gripped the wheel tighter and looked slantwise at Dan to see if the comment was delivered with malice, rather than just a simple statement.

"I don't get to see them much in my line of work." Marlow never voiced her feelings to anyone, and hadn't intended to start now, but found she suddenly had a case of verbal diarrhoea. "In fact, I haven't seen them for just over two years. My husband... ex-husband, Trebor, does his very best to keep them away."

Dan whistled low between his teeth. "Wow, you must have been a terrible mother."

Again Marlow glanced at the kid and saw his eyes were wide with interest as he studied her, as if trying to peel away the layers of unkemptness to see what lay underneath. Marlow stole a second glance, searching for any signs of a smug smile, but saw nothing.

"I don't think I was," she said defensively.

"Then why don't they want to see you? If you were my mum then... OK, bad example. If I knew where my dad was, I'd be desperate to see him."

Marlow pondered this for a moment. All her problems had been squarely focused on Trebor. She'd assumed she'd been the perfect wife and mother, and Trebor had been the cuckoo who had disrupted the family nest. Of course, he had always blamed her, but now Marlow wondered if there was something in that. She had always blamed her dad for embroiling her in the family business, which she had seen as drawing her focus away from the life she yearned to lead.

"You blame everybody but yourself," said Dan sagely, and with a jaded voice, as he followed the windscreen wipers batting hypnotically side-to-side.

Marlow gave him a sharp elbow in the ribs - partly to stop him from sleeping but mostly for the impudence of vocalising her own thoughts.

Dan blinked, aware he was on the edge of slumber. For the first time his own fear was keeping his narcolepsy at bay. He licked his dry lips, searching for something else to say.

"So what happened to your dad?"

"What d'you mean?" asked Marlow, keeping her eyes on the road as she too fought sleep.

"Well, you inherited the family business even though you didn't want to and you're all alone fighting these things. So I kinda thought..." Uncharacteristically Dan paused, searching for the words.

"You thought what?"

"I thought, y'know, he must have bought the farm." Dan looked impassive, despite the realisation that it was a terrible phrase to use. "Dead," he amended. After a long pause, he added detail: "Swallowed whole by some terrible nightmare while trying to save some poor kid. A heroic sort of death."

Marlow laughed - it was dry and humourless, and Dan preferred it when she was being snarky. She pounded the wheel with the palm of her left hand.

"A hero? My Pa? You gotta be kidding. He retired. Threw the entire damn business in my lap. My lap, not my sister's, ignoring the fact I had no interest in helping people like..." she faltered and waved her hand in Dan's direction.

"Like me," prompted Dan flatly. "Freaks who dream unlike the freaks who can't," he added snidely.

Marlow sobered up. "Yeah. Exactly. He travelled the world a bit. Never checked if I was okay, alive, had all my limbs attached. Nothing. He doesn't care, he just wanted to retire and study. Turned his back on everything. Turned his back on me." Marlow lapsed into a silence only broken by the jarring engine and the screech of windshield wipers smudging snow. "Last I heard, he had a cottage somewhere in Cornwall. Never told me; never sent so much as a Christmas card."

"Maybe he was waiting for you to get in touch?"

"You're just a kid. What d'you know?"

Dan stiffened in his seat. "Yes. You're perfectly right. What would I know? If our places were swapped, I would be asking for help and advice, but you're the adult. You know best."

Marlow's cheeks burned, although she wasn't certain if it was with anger or embarrassment. Locking horns with Dan's logic, she was out of her league. It was made all the worse because his answers so happened to be useful. How dare he.

Dan yawned, his mouth extending so wide his jaw clicked.

"I'm feeling exhausted. I don't think I can keep awake much longer."

Half a mile back, Marlow had seen signs for a lay-by, so within a minute they had pulled over in the dark parking area. It was an unlit place, surrounded by dense forest. Dan was already asleep before Marlow stopped the engine. Fearing an immanent attack in the confined space of the Beetle, she snatched the kit bag from the back seat and climbed out into the snow. The air was still frigid but at least the snow was petering out and being outside was better than being close to the boy as he slept, plus the cold gave her a second wind against the fatigue that was making her limbs feel heavy.

She took the night-vision goggles from the bag and strapped them on her head. They were heavy, probably a decade out of date, but at least they worked. Worn padding weighed on her nose; the lenses gave a faint whine of servomotors as they struggled to adjust focus. As she flicked the switch on the side of the helmet, the blackness was immediately flooded with blues, greys and greens as the details hidden in the night reveal itself. The car's engine and exhaust pipe emitted ghostly white halos caused by the heat they generated. A red and orange Dan was clearly defined in the car, rolled onto his side, face pressed against the window in, his slow deep breaths fogging the window.

Marlow crouched and swept her gaze under the car, then to the trees lining the lay-by. Infiltrators didn't generate body heat, quite the reverse, but the goggles would give her a slight advantage against the darkness. Nothing lurking in the fringes of reality.

She sighed and shivered, knowing that she would have to rest at some point. There were only so many hours a person could do without sleep before going insane, and she was unsure which side of that barrier she was on. But what could she do?

Sleeping anywhere near Dan was dangerous. The Infiltrators would go straight for her - the largest threat they faced. Conversely, she couldn't leave Dan alone to fend for himself. Sure, the kid would be okay, but Marlow wasn't optimistic for anyone else's survival rate.

And the Infiltrators... Dan could uniquely generate more than one and in the daytime too. Marlow shivered, this time not from the cold. The sheer size of the thing in the service station was terrifying. Every indication was a portent that something major was happening, but Marlow had no clue what it could be. The problem was that she had nobody to turn to. Whatever was going to happen, she was alone.

Alone...

She flinched when something moved in the trees. She slowly drew the baseball bat from the bag and cautiously approached the dark woods.

DAN WOKE FEELING fresher than ever. He blinked the sleep from his eyes and gave a long yawn as he glanced around the empty car. The windows were fogged and there was no sign of Marlow. With the ignition off, the car's clock was blank, so he had no idea what time it was.

Stepping from the car offered no further clues. A soft fog clung to the road and drifted through the trees, giving the scene a dreamlike quality. That was a worry. If he couldn't tell the difference between dreaming and reality...

"Marlow?" the fog swallowed his voice. He licked his cracked lips and tried a little louder. "Marlow? Where are you?"

Silence.

Dan felt his stomach lurch, not from hunger, but from the prospect of being abandoned in the middle of nowhere. To his own surprise, the prospect of not having Marlow around worried him.

"Marlow, stop messing around!"

He scrambled around the car, heart beating faster. There was no sign of the woman. Surely she wouldn't have abandoned him?

Of course she would, nagged a voice at the back of his mind. *She abandoned her own kids, hadn't she? You're on your own, Danny-boy.*

Dan yanked the driver's door open and saw the keys still dangling from the ignition. If Marlow was going to do a runner then wouldn't she have left Dan somewhere and took the car? That made little sense. Unless...

Despite the chill air, Dan felt a cold hand grasp him from within. *Unless she was dead...*

The thought rattled him. *He* would be responsible, just like he was responsible for all the other monstrosities.

"Marlow?" he couldn't keep the anguish from his voice. He turned, shouting to the trees - then he saw something that made his dark thoughts edge towards reality. Marlow's half-open kit bag lay behind the car. The blunderbuss was on top. That sealed it - Marlow wouldn't have willingly left the gun.

Dan ran to the bag, tears numbing his cheeks. This had to be a dream.

It had to be...

The fog swirled. The silence was complete.

Then... he spun around, his eyes combing the trees, trying to locate the growl he thought he'd heard. His own breathing seemed deafening, so he held his breath and listened.

There - coming from the trees, the unmistakable growl of a Nightmare.

Dan took a step towards it. He was unarmed, but if the beast was going to spring and end it all... so be it.

Branches cracked under his trainers as he stepped beyond the line of trees. "Here I am! Come and get me!"

The growl was nearer. Dan turned to his right. It was definitely close... then a thought struck him. If the Infiltrators could only appear when he was asleep, how could they hang around when he was awake?

He took a step towards the noise. Another grunt drew his attention to a low bush. Dan felt his heart in his mouth; his legs trembled as he took a hesitant step forward. Leaves as dry as paper crunched underfoot. His fingers wrapped around a long branch on the floor. They were so cold they were almost numb, and he could only feel the wood when he gripped it tightly. He raised his cudgel, knowing that a thin spear would do little to defend him, but it made him feel secure.

Another snort. Was the beast readying to pounce?

Dan girded his courage and swung the branch down as hard as he could into the foliage. He was rewarded with a sharp thud as it broke in two. A pained howl came from the bush as the fowl-smelling creature bounded out.

"What the hell're you doing?" it roared.

Dan hastily backed, tripping over the uneven ground and landed on his butt in the mud. Marlow loomed over him, straggling vegetation hanging from her wild hair. She looked almost as confused as Dan.

"M-Marlow?" stuttered Dan. "Are you real?"

"You better bloody believe it!" Marlow reached a hand around to her shoulder to rub where Dan had struck her. "What the hell were you thinking?"

Dan stood, wiping the mud from his backside. The wet was already seeping through to his underwear. "You were snoring like a monster."

"I don't snore," snapped Marlow.

"Just like you don't dream," replied Dan with a smirk.

"I must have nodded off." She glanced at her watch and muttered under her breath. She took a few strides out of the woods and was relieved to see the car was in one piece.

"Don't worry," said Dan following her, "no nightmare popped out to steal your precious car."

He didn't see Marlow give him a curious slantwise glance as she scooped up the bag and gun. Leaving equipment haphazardly around wasn't her style. She tried to recall her movements and could only imagine that she must have fallen asleep mid-step.

"C'mon, we should keep moving," she said, shoving the bag into the boot. "Especially now I'm awake enough to drive."

"Where too?"

Marlow opened the car door, but leaned on the roof, drumming dirty fingers thoughtfully. If she didn't dream, then Dan thought there was little chance that the sleep had given her a chance to work up a plan. That would take imagination. Dan's stomach grumbled so loudly that Marlow flinched, thinking that the boy had fallen asleep.

"I think breakfast would be the smartest move."

IT TOOK them just under an hour to find a roadside restaurant. It was half full, the parking area dotted with cars and trucks. They sat in a booth as a middle-aged waitress took their order while industriously chewing gum. Marlow ordered a full English breakfast and Dan's mouth had already started watering when he saw the menu's picture of a pancake tower smothered in maple syrup. A hanging television played the morning news in the corner of the room. A silence fell between them. This time not an uncomfortable one, but one of acceptance. They didn't speak until after the food arrived.

Marlow clicked her fingers to get Dan's attention.

"Huh?" Dan managed through a mouthful of pancake.

"Our next step?"

Dan tried to recall the conversation, but he had totally zoned out, so shook his head blankly.

Marlow sighed heavily and stabbed a fork into the leathery bacon. "I was saying we need to work out our next step. We can't keep running like this. Especially since the Infiltrators are following *you* wherever you go. And I need sleep. Desperately need sleep. I can't keep doing this."

"OK." Dan gave an expectant silence but Marlow didn't fill it. "So what do we do?" he finally asked.

Marlow stared at the food, absently chasing a rouge baked bean with her fork. "No idea," she finally admitted. "This is a little out of my experience. I mean, the usual Infiltrator cases are dealt with swiftly, violently and, more importantly, closed, after my first visit. You're being targeted for a reason." Dan looked away as Marlow's gaze bore into him as if she was searching for answers inside his head. Dan focused on the TV again. "It can't just be the narcolepsy. I can't believe that. I mean, other people are afflicted with that, but they don't suffer like you."

Marlow's voice became a soft drone. Dan's eyelids fluttered before his brain suddenly kicked in, screaming at him to stay alert. His head jerked as he caught himself nodding off. He sighed heavily - that was a close call. Marlow didn't seem to have noticed, her monologue was addressed firmly at her food. Dan rubbed his eyes and looked back at the screen.

"Why're we on TV?" Dan suddenly asked with a hint of alarm.

It took a few moments for Marlow to register the comment. She followed Dan's gaze to the screen. The picture was split between a smiling photo of Dan, taken at the end of term in school, and an unsmiling, slightly out-of-focus picture

of Marlow scowling at the camera. She was just about recognisable with her hair tied back in a smart ponytail, and the
clothes actually fitted.

"What the hell...?" Marlow began. She didn't recognise the
picture, but it had undoubtedly come from her ex. They hadn't
even Photoshopped out the jagged line from where he had
torn it in half, so it looked as if Marlow had no neck.

The TV was muted and Marlow didn't dare attract
anyone's attention by asking them to turn the volume up, but
the scrolling chyron at the bottom told them everything they
needed to know.

Dan Glass. Kidnapped. Marlow Cornelius suspected.
Nationwide manhunt.

Dan giggled. "Kidnapped? Cool! Where'd they get an idea
like that?"

Marlow was staring at the screen, utterly appalled. Her
usual pale features were, if possible, whiter than ever. When
Dan looked back at the report, he gasped when he saw his
mum sobbing in front of the camera. The brief spark of
amusement now thoroughly snubbed. Her words were silent,
but the anguish and tears rolling down her cheeks spoke
volumes. His Grandpa stood behind, a hand on her shoulder as
he stared at his feet. Dan felt his heart wrench.

"My God! They think I've kidnapped you!" hissed Marlow.
She tried to angle her body in the booth and kept her head
bowed to avoid eye contact with the other diners.

"Why would they think that? Grandpa paid you to find me,
didn't he?"

That was exactly what Marlow was wondering. She stared
at Grandpa Boris. He was looking anywhere except at his own
daughter or into the camera. Reading the guilt on his face was
like reading a subtitle written in a very large bold font.
Marlow's mind was racing.

"You bastard... your Grandpa..."

"What about him?"

"He didn't tell your mother!"

"What're you talking about?"

"Boris came to my house and pleaded with me to search for you." She recalled details of their hungover meeting. "Your mother wasn't around. He hadn't told her you were missing!"

Dan frowned. "Why would he do that?"

Marlow hesitated. She had no idea why he wouldn't simply tell her the truth. Why would he claim Marlow had kidnapped Dan? That didn't make any sense.

"Right. We're heading straight back so you can explain this mix up to them."

Marlow stood up, but Dan made no move to follow.

"Come on," Marlow insisted.

Dan desperately wanted to return home to put his mother's mind at ease, but what would he be returning to?

"Dan, this is no time for messing around," Marlow warned. She felt as if her patience was being tested, but Dan refused to move. He slunk back into the booth, shielding his face with one hand to avoid being identified. Marlow spoke in a hissing whisper that was on the verge of erupting into full-blown anger. "This is serious!"

Dan nodded, his jumbled thoughts slowly reaching his lips. "I know. If we go back... it's the same problem, isn't it?" Marlow blinked in surprise. Being branded a kidnapper had momentarily obscured the fact that the boy was pulling dark creatures from the abyss of another dimension that readily killed. Dan toyed with his half-full glass of cola. From where he was sitting, it was half empty. "The Nightmares will still come." He nodded towards the television. "Their lives will still be at risk, won't they?"

Fatigue was fogging Marlow's thoughts. If she returned the

boy home, and his mother and grandpa were killed by a blood-thirsty Infiltrator, then she would be complicit in their deaths. Was that worse than being arrested as a kidnapper?

Yes! She berated herself. With a horrible twisting sensation in her gut, Marlow realised she was *responsible,* not only for the kid's safety but of those around him. She tried to imagine explaining the Infiltrators to the cops. A *mentally unstable* kidnapper, she amended.

Out of the corner of her eyes she noticed their waitress was leaning through the hatch, in heated discussions with the cook. Their glance darted between the screen and Marlow as they spoke. They'd been recognised.

"Dan, listen. We gotta get out of here. I think our waitress has called the cops." She just blown her tip, Marlow thought bitterly.

"I'm not going home," said Dan definitely.

"If the cops get us, then you'll have no choice!" hissed Marlow, panic mounting.

They stared at one another, neither willing to back down. Marlow's steely gaze broke first when she heard approaching police sirens.

"Dan..."

"You promise to help me?"

Marlow banged the table in frustration, gaining unwelcome attention from the other diners. She didn't care; there was no point in remaining anonymous now.

"What can I do?"

"Stop the Nightmares. Stop them for good and I'll get us out of this right now."

Questions piled in Marlow's mind, but the squeal of rubber outside and the cold blue strobes of police lights sucked up all his attention. Two cars had pulled up, the officers climbing out as a police van skidded to a halt behind them. Marlow watched in dismay as armed cops leapt out, lethal snub-nosed rifles in hand.

Christ, they were fast...

"Do we have a deal?" asked Dan, extending his hand.

Marlow hated herself, but hated the kid more. She had no other choice than to shake Dan's hand. Her voice cracked as she spoke. "Deal."

"This is the police! Marlow Cornelius, we know you're in there with the boy - come out with your hands up or we will be forced to enter!"

Marlow's blood ran cold. "Whatever you're gonna tell them, now's your chance." Dan said nothing. "Kid, don't screw around."

Marlow switched her gaze from the cops to the boy. Her heart sank. Dan was slumped on the table, head cradled across his arms; fast asleep.

"Okay, Cornelius. We're coming in. Five..."

Marlow felt every eye in the diner on her at the same time people sank beneath their tables, eager to avoid being caught in any crossfire.

"...Four..."

Marlow stood. She knew it was futile to put up any form of defence - especially since she was innocent. She had done nothing except agree to help the kid's annoying Grandpa.

"...Three..."

Counter-thoughts raced through her mind. Whatever she said to the authorities would sound like delirious ramblings. She had no choice but to run. Her eyes swept from the front entrance, where police strobes blinded her, to the kitchen door. No doubt the cops would have people positioned out back.

The lights in the diner suddenly flickered - then extinguished. Marlow had watched enough films to know the police would cut the power before storming the building.

This was it. All she had to do was make sure she didn't get shot.

"...Tw-eeeeekkk...."

The cop's voice turned into a wet gurgle over the loud-speaker. Then screams rose from outside, followed by the rapid dull crack of automatic gunfire. With the diner lights off, Marlow's eyes quickly adjusted to the darkness beyond - just enough to see a huge slimy limb coiled around a police car and hoist it into the air, complete with a screaming cop inside.

Seconds later, a severed half of the car was hurled through the front of the building in a colossal shower of glass. People inside yelled as they darted aside. The vehicle crushed several empty booths. Diners fled in panic - some fled through the broken windows, while other shoved through the kitchen door.

Two people made it outside, Marlow recalled that they were a couple that had been giving her particularly surly looks. They were instantly set upon by a cat-like creature the size of a small family car. Where its head should be was a swirling mass of tentacles resembling a sea anemone. They scrambled away, out of sight as the beast pursued them.

Marlow realised that she still had her hands raised in surrender. Feeling foolish, she looked at Dan, awestruck. The boy had intentionally opened the rift between Innerspace, allowing the creatures to come flooding through.

Creatures.

Marlow marvelled, now the kid was channelling more than one Infiltrator. The boy was safe, but everybody around him, including Marlow, was at risk. Marlow was impressed by the kid's gutsy move, while another part of her felt pure terror at the size and quantity of Infiltrators the boy was channelling.

Three cops charged past the diner, taking potshots at something pursuing them. Nine stilt-like legs, covered in sharp thorns, scuttled past moments later. Marlow was grateful the beast's grotesque body remained out of sight.

Something exploded outside, kicking Marlow back to her own precarious situation. She could flee, leaving the boy here, knowing that he at least would be immune from the Infiltrators. She could probably build enough of a head start to avoid capture, at least for a few days.

She took several steps around the half-police car, which had landed on its roof trapping the cops inside, then looked back at Dan. The boy was sweating, although oblivious to the real-life nightmare, it looked as if he was suffering one himself. Normally an Infiltrator would feed pleasant dreams to the conduit to keep them asleep, but Marlow wondered if channelling this many creatures would taint the anaesthetic. From the looks of it, Dan was suffering terribly.

If she left, then what? The kid would be reunited to a fretful mother and despicable Grandpa only to unleash yet more Nightmares and death. Marlow took another step to the gaping window and experienced a very rare feeling: an epiphany.

She had promised to help the boy. Promised he wouldn't be taken home until his 'problem' had been cured.

"Dammit!"

Marlow's curse echoed through the now empty diner and was met by a chatter of automatic gunfire. Seconds later, a police van was hurled across the car park. Something roared - it clearly didn't belong in this world, although it sounded happy to be here.

Marlow hurried back to Dan and hoisted him over her shoulder. Heat radiated from the limp boy as if he was enduring a terrible fever.

"Okay, kid, time to get you outta here. Keep it up just a little longer and pray you're not getting people killed."

She ran for the window. The boy was so light he wasn't a burden. She gingerly poked her head out and saw more cops across the car park cowering behind dumpsters as the cat-mare stood on top of a vehicle, powerful limbs crushing the metal. With dismay, Marlow recognised it was her beloved Beetle.

She ran across the car park with no actual plan other than to put distance between them. A policeman wearing full protective body armour suddenly blocked her path. Marlow froze - the game was up.

Then she saw the fear on the cop's face and, before a word could be uttered, something like a strand of green slime adhered to the cop's back and he was violently plucked upwards into the air, arms and legs flailing.

Marlow changed direction. Ahead, a new BMW had its engine running. The side window was smashed and whoever had been in it had been extracted by force. Marlow didn't want to think about it too much. She threw Dan in the back. His head hit the padded seat with a bump that would wake anybody else, but he simply snorted and drooled as he continued experiencing his own private nightmare.

Marlow slipped behind the wheel and mashed the accelerator. The BMW roared across the car park. She veered around fleeing diners, including the traitorous waitress who was being pursued by something that ran human-like on two legs. Marlow's initial *schadenfreude* was snuffed by remorse about what would happen if she was caught.

She jerked the wheel and ran the rat-human over with a sickening crunch. The Beamer's front grill snapped and twisted, the bonnet crumpling as icy blue blood splattered across the windscreen.

"Wake up, kid!" she yelled. "You gotta stop this. It's gone too far!"

Dan remained asleep. They bounced over a speed bump with such force the suspension creaked ominously. Marlow's head cracked against the roof, but Dan remained asleep.

"WAKE UP!"

Marlow skidded the car a hard ninety-degrees. Dan slid across the rear seat and smashed his head against the door. He remained asleep. As they pulled out of the diner, Marlow wondered if channelling so many creatures had thrown him into a coma. The whole situation was unlike any she had experienced before. It was new and frightening, and she knew drastic action would be required.

She glanced in the mirror as they jounced onto the road; gunfire flickered in the darkness behind them. If Dan wouldn't wake, then Marlow could only hope distance would severe the Conduit link before it killed everybody.

CHAPTER ELEVEN

DAN JOLTED awake with a cry as frigid water splashed over him. He thought he was drowning and all he could see were blurs as another cold jet of water splashed him between the eyes.

"Wow! Stop!"

"Sorry," grunted Marlow's familiar drawl, "Didn't see you'd opened your eyes."

Dan groped for his glasses and felt them thrust into his hand. He was feeling disoriented and a little sick. Marlow's face hove into view. Her usual surly expression replaced with concern.

"Where are we?"

Dan took stock of his surroundings. It was daylight. He was lying on the back seat of a rather expensive car that was now sopping wet. He sat up and the world swam around him. He gripped the back of the passenger seat for support.

Events from that morning flooded into his memory. The police had turned up thinking that Marlow had kidnapped him. He recalled his desperation at the thought of being

returned home and the deal he'd made with Marlow. She had
had little choice but to agree, so Dan instantly allowed himself
to be swallowed into the welcoming embrace of sleep that had
been gnawing at him for hours.

"What happened?" He dreaded the answer.

"You're full of questions this afternoon," grunted Marlow
leaning through the window as she chucked a Mars bar at him.
"You sorted the cops out, that's for sure."

Dan smiled as he peeled open the bar. He bit into it and
noticed Marlow didn't look like a woman that was thankful for
being saved.

"They're alright, aren't they?" asked Dan as he chewed.
Marlow's expression made him hesitate. At the same time he
recalled the unpleasant nightmare he'd experienced; the first
he could ever remember having. In it, he was running through
a dark unpleasant landscape unaccountably heading towards an
ancient arena, a twisted obsidian structure that was home to a
colossal creature that broadcast tangible malice. He could
recall nothing more than a blob of flailing limbs with a hideous
slit-like mouth running the length of its tower blocked sized
body. Its skin constantly blistered and popped, spawning the
creatures that Infiltrated people's dreams. Dan shivered at the
thought.

"Well, let's just say that they no longer think I'm just a
kidnapper," sighed Marlow.

"Good," Dan said automatically before he had a chance to
process the statement. "What do you mean 'just'?"

"A lot of people..." Marlow's voice trailed off. She coughed
and couldn't meet Dan's eyes. "They think I, somehow, killed
some of those people back there. Despite the evidence... they
think I did it." Marlow shook her head and Dan felt uncomfortable. "It's getting outta control, kid. You're like a nuclear

meltdown, building 'n' building until pop." She made an explosive gesture.

The chocolate in Dan's mouth was suddenly tasteless, but he swallowed it anyway. Marlow looked like somebody who had already been convicted, and Dan knew that it was his fault. He had destroyed her life. He was responsible for the atrocities at the diner. If it wasn't for him, everything would have been all right.

"I promised to help you, kid," she said slowly. "Truth is... I don't know how to."

"You mean you'd be better off if I wasn't around?"

Marlow laughed, humourlessly. "Right. Then what?" Her gaze turned as hard as steel. "You know... all my life I've been running from things. People... my dad, my ex... hell, even my own kids. Know what that makes me?"

Dan shrugged and once again his mouth worked faster than his ability to edit what he said. "A loser?" he instantly regretted saying it and was surprised to see her nodding.

"You know, kid, you're honest. Not many people are and without that... how can you trust people?"

Dan clamped his mouth shut, certain that silence was the best policy. He was certain, *almost certain*, that Marlow had just slipped him a compliment.

Marlow cracked her knuckles and continued with a bemused smile. "A loser. I never saw that coming. No matter how much I hated the family business, I saw a way out. I had a goal, plans. I wasn't gonna get stuck like my old man. That's what I thought. Still did... drinking myself to death, avoiding my own family. No wonder they never want to see me. Look at me!" She slammed a fist on the roof.

Dan wasn't afraid, he knew she was simply venting anger and after all they had been through, he couldn't blame her. He couldn't guess what emotions were violently cycling through her head. "All my life I have been running. I thought I was running *to* something. Turns out I was running away. You think I'm gonna let you go and suffer through this on your own? Yesterday, sure, what the hell. Today, no. Different story. Different tune. Different me. It's time to grab life by the neck an' grab back the bad hand we've been dealt!"

With each sentence her voice rose passionately. Dan felt inspired with each word until they were both smiling.

"How?" he asked, voice breaking with enthusiasm.

Marlow punched the sky, a wide grin cracking her face. "I ain't got no idea!"

FOR THE REST of the day they drove in thoughtful silence. Dan tried to concentrate on the passing landscape, which was nothing but snowy winter hills. With little of interest to see, he was constantly fighting fatigue. Only the thought of what had happened at the diner chilled him enough to stay awake. Marlow had bought eight energy drinks, but they were churning Dan's stomach to the point of inducing constant nausea. Each time he felt he was drifting into an unwelcome narcoleptic embrace, he focused on his mother, forcing her image to appear in his minds-eye. An image of sadness and despair. He couldn't even remember her smile. It was enough to keep him semi-alert, although he was fighting a losing battle.

Marlow occasionally turned the radio on to listen to the news. There was nothing further about the murdering kidnapper, but it did little to sway her fears. Out in a country lane they had passed a lone police car and had both held their breath, more than aware they were in a stolen car... but it passed without incident.

They kept to winding country roads and Marlow hadn't

spoken about their destination and Dan hadn't asked, although Marlow became increasingly grim with each mile they passed.

When Dan's head began to fog, he did his usual trick of biting his tongue hard. The jolt was enough to wake him, but he needed some sort of interaction to stay alert.

"Tell me about your kids."

Marlow blinked as if Dan had just woken her.

"My kids... well, uh, I got two of them."

"Wow. Sounds like you really got to know them."

Marlow scowled, but the look quickly became thoughtful as she glanced at Dan.

"Molly and Jamie. Molly's the youngest. She's funny, always laughing, never sad. She had a cheeky sparkle in her eye the day she was born." Marlow laughed at some private memory. As Dan watched, the clouds of gloomy frustration vaporised from her face and, for the first time, Dan saw a look of caring. "Every Sunday I'd take her horse riding. She loved that. I mean, really loved it. All week she'd get excited, read books about it, y'know. And she took to it like a... like a professional. She'd stop laughing. The concentration in her eyes... that was something beyond pure joy."

Dan wanted to ask more questions, but he was afraid of breaking the fragile mask of joy Marlow was exhibiting.

"Jamie's 'bout your age. He's a real dreamer too." She shot a look at Dan, but there was something odd in the expression. It took Dan several moments to realise that the oddness was the lack of bitterness he'd become accustomed to. "He don't take after me."

"Thank God for that!" said Dan before he could censor his words. To his surprise, Marlow laughed.

"Yep. Thank God. He's an explorer. Always getting where he shouldn't be. Always looking for something new. Fascinated by everything."

"I always wanted to be an explorer. Loved looking at maps of the world. My dad used to get me encyclopaedias..." His voice cracked at the mention of his father. That was something he never thought about, other than in a cloud of sadness. Out of the corner of his eye, he saw Marlow give him an inquisitive look. Dan cleared his throat and continued. "I used to love looking through them. See what the world was really like. Then he left. Grandpa told me the world's already been explored. That there's nothing new left to discover and that I should stay home and focus on something real."

To Dan's surprise, Marlow slapped the rim of the steering wheel and scoffed derisively. "Your Grandpa's a dolt! There's so much left to explore. You know only about 5% of the oceans have been explored? Who knows what's lurking in there? Y'know, they still find animals unknown to science every year. Space... that's the entire universe waiting to be investigated. Then there's Innerspace," she tapped his head. "Your dreams allow you to pass multiple dimensions. Peek into dimensions that no one else can." Marlow shook her head and looked genuinely angry. "Boris doesn't know what he's talking about. Never let anyone tell ya there's nothing left to discover. They're the ignorant ones."

Dan regarded Marlow with surprise. He would never have pegged her to have a caring bone in her body, yet here she was defending him.

"My Jamie's gonna do exactly what he wants to do. Nobody'll be able to stand in his way, you'll see. He'll make epic discoveries." Marlow lapsed into thoughtful silence, only speaking up when they reached a sharp junction and she turned the wheel around a tight arc. "Just wish I could be there to see it," she mumbled under her breath.

"Why don't you give them a call? I bet they'd love to hear from you."

"Huh. My Tree won't let me near them. He thinks I'm a bad influence."

Dan fished his mobile phone from his pocket. It was still switched off in case his family tried to make contact. He waved it so close to Marlow's face that she swatted at it.

"Why don't you call them now?"

"Don't be stupid."

"I bet they'd love to hear from you." He saw a flicker of temptation as Marlow glanced at the phone. "I could call and ask for them, if you're worried your ex will answer." Again he danced the phone tantalisingly.

Marlow gripped the wheel harder. "Forget it."

"You're not making the effort," Dan said indignantly. "They don't have a choice if you're around or not. That choice is *yours,* and I think that's unfair."

"You don't think I try?" there was a trace of astonishment to Marlow's voice. "I try..."

"Like when? Sorry, but if you were my mum and came to the house looking like that, I'd run a mile!" He tried to suppress a yawn as he met Marlow's gaze. She was forced to turn away to focus on the road. "You smell," he clarified.

"I don't..."

"You smell like a wet dog threw up in a brewery, then peed on itself!"

Marlow opened her mouth to disagree, but Dan continued.

"No wonder the police are after you, you look like the sort of psychopath a psycho would stay away from!"

"I ain't had no opportunity for a pamper since you crawled into my life," snapped Marlow.

Dan suddenly felt the car swim and he yawned. "Sometimes life's unfair..."

Then he slipped into a sudden deep sleep.

· · ·

I T WAS dark when Dan awoke. The first thing he noticed was that they were still driving. The second was that the car had grown a sunroof through which he could see stars gleaming between the patchwork of snow-heavy clouds. Odd, he didn't recall the car having one.

Wake up, focus, he told himself.

He could feel the cool breeze through the sunroof which meant it wasn't glass. Then he finally got it. The front half of the roof had been removed. He could see the jagged scars from where it had been torn off. The windshield was heavily cracked and poked by blossoms of white spider-webbed cracks. The dashboard in front of Dan had fractured and, alarmingly, melted in places. Only the pine cone air freshener dangling from the mirror assured him it was the same vehicle.

He could see Marlow's silhouette as she drove in the darkness, and only when a car passed and cast its headlights across them, did he see a new cherry-red scar on her cheek.

"You're bleeding!"

Marlow glanced at him. "Awake at last? Boy, you were deep. Couldn't do nothing to wake ya."

"Is it getting worse?" Marlow's silence was confirmation enough. "What happened?"

"You sent an Infiltrator to remodel the car. Damn near bit my head off too."

Dan felt a flush of guilt. "I'm s-sorry," he stammered.

Marlow clumsily patted him on the shoulder, and in doing so sucked heavily through her teeth to stifle the pain from another scar that ran down her arm, cutting through the heavy jacket.

"Ain't your fault, kid."

"What're we going to do?"

"First, gotta stop that narcolepsy, slow it down at least. That's just perfect for Them. It looks like you're in some kinda coma straight after too. I bet they're doing something new to keep you under longer. You had any dreams?"

Dan thought hard. He was used to the pleasant dreams, which he now knew came from the Infiltrators' anaesthetic, and the previous night's terror was something he had never experienced before. But the last sleep... he could remember nothing. Nothing at all in fact which was unusual enough. He shook his head.

"Mmmm, they're doing something alright," said a thoughtful Marlow.

"So what can we do?"

Marlow took a deep breath and held it before speaking again. "I know someone who can help."

"Who? I thought you were the only one who did... this. You know, fought Nightmares."

Marlow looked gravely at Dan. "There is somebody else."

Dan shook his head. He couldn't guess what Marlow meant.

With a sigh, Marlow cracked her neck to the side and then told him. Dan was thankful he still had his seatbelt on because he was sure he would have fallen from the moving car in surprise.

CHAPTER TWELVE

GRAVEL CRUNCHED under the tyres as they pulled up the long driveway. It was still dark, and Dan was craning to make anything out. It had also begun to snow heavily, and it drifted through the open roof, stinging them both in the face.

"Are you sure this is the right place?" he asked. Marlow grunted in acknowledgement. "I didn't see any signs. When were you last here? How long ago since you last saw him? He could have moved."

Marlow said nothing, but gently guided the car up the winding driveway. She guessed that Dan had expected a grandiose mansion at the end because of his disappointed huff when the headlights drifted across a crumbling cottage. Vines clung to the walls with such ferocity it looked as if the building would collapse if they were ever cut away. Dust and grime covered the windows, making them dark and mysterious. The only sign of life was the wisp of smoke curling from the chimney, caught in the very edge of the headlights.

"This is right," growled Marlow quietly as they climbed

from the car. With no engine running it was deathly quiet, save the unblemished snow crunching underfoot.

Dan fidgeted nervously as he downed yet another energy drink. "Soooo... do we just knock?"

He took three steps towards the house when all hell broke loose. Blinding lights erupted all around them, burning from concealed places. A piercing siren WHOOPED, followed by a loud voice.

"You are trespassing! Turn around and leave immediately or force will gladly be used!"

Dan dropped his drink and thrust his hands in the air, frantically looking in every direction.

"Don't shoot! Don't shoot!" he yelled.

Marlow leaned against the car's bonnet with a half-smile. She shook her head knowingly.

"We come in peace!" yelled Dan dropping to his knees. "Don't shoot!"

The siren suddenly wound down with a pathetic gurgle. There was movement against the lights, nothing more than an abstract silhouette. Dan shielded his eyes to get a better look.

"Marlow...?" came a croaky voice from the shadows.

A man stepped into view. Thick round glasses balanced on a bulbous nose. His pure white hair combed back at the temples and his face was weather-beaten and old, with a bushy white moustache clinging to his upper lip. He stood just a little taller than Dan, in part due to his slightly hunched posture, which was no doubt dragged down by the weight of the solid duel-barrel shotgun he was carrying. Unlike Marlow's blunderbuss, this had one barrel above the other, a marksman's weapon.

"Marlow Cornelius?"

Marlow spoke, but her first words came in a dry hack. She cleared her throat and tried again. "Dad."

Carlos Cornelius stepped forward, his eyes locked on Marlow. The gun swung limply from one hand while the other brushed over his hair in a disbelieving manner.

"Well, bless my... I..." His eyes finally swung away from Marlow and studied Dan, who was still kneeling on the gravel, one hand raised, the other shielding his eyes. "And is this... Jamie?"

"No, dad. This is Dan and he definitely isn't one of mine." Marlow cleared her throat again and looked sheepish. "We really need your help."

DAN'S TEETH still chattered as he sat in front of the open log fire. After everything they had been through, the warmth was still avoiding him. Nothing had been said when Marlow's father had guided them inside and positioned them in front of the fire. He stoked the logs, increasing the ferocity of the flames, then furnished them with cups of hot cocoa. Dan took one sip of the heavenly velvet drink before Marlow whipped it from his hands and replaced it with a bitter black coffee.

Carlos had tended to Marlow's recent wounds. Rust tarnished the needle, but the care he took in sewing up her wounds was done with marked precision. There was no small talk between father and daughter, just curiosity, and occasional disbelieving glances from them both when they thought the other wasn't looking. Only when they had settled in front of the fire had Marlow's father said: "Well..." did Marlow suddenly relay the entire chain of events in a torrent of information in which she seldom paused to suck in breath. It was evident that she had been running the conversation through her mind during the entire trip and wanted to get it all out to justify their arrival. By the end of the story, Marlow and her father were both staring at Dan. The crackling flames reflecting from the old man's thick glasses were mesmeric.

"That is a tale, no doubt," said the old man, tugging at his moustache thoughtfully. "I never heard the like."

"So what can we do?" asked Marlow.

"Well... the boy is certainly fascinating. He would make for an interesting study..."

"The boy's right in front of you," barked Dan. "And he's tired, peed off, and just wants a peaceful night's sleep killing nobody. And he really, really wants to go back home."

The man's eyes grew to saucers - then he broke into an infectious laugh until tears streamed from his eyes. He repeatedly slapped his knee to calm down. Despite his irritation, Dan couldn't help but smile.

"Forgive an old soul, Daniel, but you really are a fascinating find. Who would have thought this lug would be the one to hook a Conduit like you?" Marlow stiffened as her father jerked a thumb in her direction.

Dan smiled. "Well, Carlos, this lug," he jerked a thumb at Marlow, ignoring her scowl, "has not only repeatedly saved my life, but the lives of dozens of others, doing what I couldn't imagine anybody else doing."

Carlos stroked his moustache thoughtfully. This time his gaze fell on Marlow as if seeing her properly for the first time. Marlow looked away feeling like a chagrined schoolgirl dragged in front of the headmaster.

"I haven't seen you for..."

"Twelve years, dad. It has been twelve years."

"Twelve years, eight months and eighteen days."

Marlow rolled her eyes. Carlos raised his hand to placate her.

"And I have felt each day, Marl."

"Marlow," Marlow automatically corrected. "You know I

hate Marl."

Dan focused the conversation back to himself. "So can you help or not?"

Carlos flashed a smile and nudged Marlow's knee. "Oh, Marl. I like this one. He has a real fire. He reminds me of..." Carlos trailed off into embarrassed silence. Marlow frowned, about to prompt him, but Carlos changed tact. "Yes... I think I may be able to help." He slapped both knees and smiled, his body quivering with more pent-up energy than a man of his age should possess. "Isn't this exciting? Finally, something new to push the brink of our understanding! I think we should brew more coffee in the pot and adjourn to the lab!"

THE LAB TURNED out to be a large greenhouse attached to the back of the cottage and extended several times over the years with no thought to match each section together and with every pane of glass obscured by filth. The air was warm and thick with heavy scents from the flora that filled it. Some plants were small, with only a few dry leaves spilling over the rim of their pots, stacked on narrow shelves. Others were huge bushy affairs, standing several feet high and trailing to the ground. Everywhere was a kaleidoscope of colourful flowers and exotic leaves. Dan admired a row of perfectly maintained bonsai.

"Got to have something to keep the old brain cells ticking," Carlos said with a smile. "Alas, I don't receive many visitors out here." His eyes darted to Marlow when he said that.

He led them to a long table at the back on which stood an elaborate network of glass tubes and beakers, all interconnected with alchemic precision. A powerful microscope was connected to a laptop. The screen was still on, indicating they had interrupted Carlos in his work. He gestured theatrically.

"The lab."

"What exactly do you do with all of this stuff?" said Dan stretching a finger towards an open Venus flytrap. Carlos swatted his hand away.

"Don't touch! I synthesise compounds extracted from these plants. Natural remedies to whatever ails us. This one," he selected a vial from a rack of a dozen others, each filled with tinted liquids, "This is almost an exact opposite hybrid of serotonin and melatonin that activates the brain's neural receptors."

"To do what?" Dan asked cautiously.

"To keep you awake without going insane," said Marlow. She picked up a flask containing electric blue liquid and swirled it. It had the constancy of jello. Carlos appeared behind her and gently pried it from her hand.

"That's a mighty rare compound." He held it up to the light, which made it appear all the brighter.

"What is it?" asked Marlow.

"An extract from a gland found within the Infiltrator's head, just behind the eyes," said Carlos in a dramatic whisper. Even Marlow leaned closer for a better look. "Believe me, it's difficult to extract. I haven't been entirely sitting on my haunches."

"What does the gland do?"

"Ah..." said Carlos uncertainly as he put the flask back on the bench. "That I don't know for sure. But I think it might be what the Infiltrators inject, or psychically inject might be a better term since I don't have the faintest idea how they do it, into their Conduit to allow them to slip between worlds. Think of it as lubrication between realities. Like oil in a car engine. Without it, the Infiltrator would just seize up and crumble. Which is why I always said, aim for the eyes." He returned to his plants.

"But you don't really know..." sighed Marlow. "Useful as ever, dad."

Carlos harrumphed and turned his attention to a plant with broad red leaves, yellow pigments outlining the veins running across the surface. Carlos whispered to it and Dan realised he was using the same tones one used to calm a stressed baby. Using a pair of tweezers, he gripped a leaf and used a scalpel to sever it from the stalk. Dropping the leaf into a petri dish, Carlos gently dabbed a cotton swab on the stalk and made shushing noises.

Dan looked at Marlow with a frown. She shook her head and spoke wistfully. "Dad thinks plants have feelings. He always talked to them. More than to his own kids."

Carlos took the petri dish and dropped the leaf into a mortar bowl. He pushed his glasses up his nose and glared at Marlow.

"Plants do have feelings. Maybe not the same as you or I, but they register a distinct electrical fluctuation when you cut them just as you would to register pain." He added a dash of water into the mortar and began to grind the leaf with a mortar. "In fact, your sister was a good listener and the plants gave me a more pleasant conversation than you did. Always complaining. Always throwing tantrums when I was giving you the greatest gift of all!" He pummelled the leaf harder and harder with each word, taking his frustrations out on it.

"Greatest gift?" Marlow spluttered. "You threw me in front of the most frightening dangers a kid would ever face – then told me how to beat them up with a baseball bat! What kinda gift is that?"

Carlos looked at his daughter with wide eyes, magnified behind his spectacles. "Knowledge, Marl. Knowledge about what lies *beyond*. Knowledge gained through generations of our family's sacrifice, defending this world from the unknown."

"I never asked for that!" snarled Marlow.

"Nobody asks for a duty like that, yet it's our honour to accept it and perform it."

"'Cause of you, I never got to dream. I never got a normal childhood. I never got nothing!"

Carlos stopped pummelling the leaf, a mixture of sorrow and surprise across his face. "Is that why...? After all these years... that's why you walked away?"

Marlow gaped, but no words came out. She sat on a stool as the messy fragments of her life slowly clashed like continents. The burn of anger was being doused by waves of self-pity, made all the worse by the recognition that her father had aged terribly in over a decade. Barely the shell of the man she remembered. She glanced at Dan and saw the boy's head was sagging, his eyes closing.

"Dan!"

Carlos reacted first, slapping Dan so hard across the face that his glasses clattered on the floor. Dan jerked awake with a yelp.

"What the what?" he exclaimed, clutching his stinging cheek.

Carlos turned back to crushing the leaf. "You must stay awake, Daniel."

Marlow examined the red mark on Dan's cheek, which was already fading. "Ah yeah. That's the old parental care I remember."

Carlos ignored her. He carefully poured the mortar's liquid contents into a glass beaker, swirled it, then placed it over a Bunsen burner. He connected a glass tube to the beaker's top, sealing it. Then he lit the Bunsen.

"What exactly are you doing?" said Dan, groping for his glasses.

"The extract is a recent little discovery of mine," Carlos

said, relieved to be diverted from the subject of his question-
able parenting. "A new orchid found in the deepest Malaysian
rain forest - I don't even think it has an official name. None
that I could find anyway, so I named it..." He drifted off in
embarrassment. He gave the glass apparatus a gentle shake to
ensure it all held together, then called up a program on the
laptop. It was a homemade database of various plants and their
effects. Dan saw a magnified image of the leaf appear on the
screen, a mass of text and molecular data underneath. He also
caught the name: *Monomeria Marlow*. Dan glanced at Marlow;
she hadn't noticed and was gently tapping the beaker as the
liquid boiled.

Carlos's tone became that of a lecturer. "Some narcolepsy is
caused by a lack of orexin..."

"I know all that," sighed Dan. "I'm not a kid."

Carlos looked at him with a frown. "Well, unless you are a
dwarf then that's exactly what you are."

"I mean, I've been through a barrage of tests to sort this
out and nothing has ever worked."

"Ah, but you have never experienced *my* juice. It generates
something very similar to orexin to prevent sleep, but works
with your other neurotransmitters to keep you feeling rela-
tively fresh and alert. Of course, your natural rhythms will
always conquer, but it should keep you on your toes. At least
for a while."

Carlos drew their attention to the beaker as a red liquid
bubbled its way along the network of tubes, losing its vivid red
colour with each distillation, until it rapidly dripped into a
second beaker the colour of a weak herbal tea.

Dan pushed his nose closer to the brew. His usual malaise
was suddenly swept away when he caught a whiff of the potent
vapours. He experienced a mixture of excitement and trepidation that his salvation lay in the bubbling tube.

It took almost an hour for the process to complete. Carlos lifted the full beaker to the light to examine the contents. Squinting, he finally gave a nod of approval. Dan grinned as he lifted the beaker up to toast Marlow, but when he looked, she was fast asleep, her grubby coat pulled tightly around her for warmth.

IT WAS STILL DARK when Marlow woke, but it felt as if she had slept for days. She seldom felt so refreshed even as she smacked her dry lips, wiped the white crud that had gathered at the corner of her mouth, and felt the overwhelming urge to drink something alcoholic.

She was still in the greenhouse and somebody had draped a blanket over her. She stood and stretched – realising that she was alone.

"Dan?" With a sudden sense of dread, Marlow darted around the greenhouse, glancing behind each shelf and down the aisle. "Dan? Where are ya?" her tension came back with the force of a sledgehammer.

Marlow ran through the kitchen: empty. Running into the corridor, her eyes swept up the staircase – then to the flickering light of a log fire coming from under the living room door. Marlow reached to open it – then hesitated. If Dan was asleep, then there was no certainty at what lay behind the door.

She patted down her coat; she was weapon-less. Marlow had seen nothing suitable in the greenhouse or the kitchen. To go in unarmed was foolhardy, but to allow Dan to sleep any longer was increasing the risks they face.

Licking her lips, and trying to stop her hand from shaking, she gripped the doorknob and gave it a slow half turn. The catch clicked and the door opened an inch. Marlow caught her breath and pushed it open. It swung back with a loud creak and the lulling warmth of a roaring log fire swept over her.

Dan sat in front of the fire, eyes open. Marlow wasn't falling for that again, the kid could still be sleeping. She tensed, ready to pounce...

Then Dan turned and smiled.

"You're finally awake," he said in a chirpy voice.

Marlow slowly entered, her eyes darting to the shadows. "You awake?"

"Um... what do you think?"

"Could be sleep talking."

Dan picked up a cushion and threw it. It was a perfect shot to Marlow's face.

"Am I sleep throwing stuff too?" said Dan with a grin. "Your father's concoction is brilliant. I don't feel tired at all. He's a genius!" His eyes gleamed as he tried to explain sensations he'd never experienced before. "It's like... like I've been asleep forever. That I have had every good night's rest I should have ever had, but all bundled into one, you know?"

Accepting the kid was awake, he was gabbling fast enough, Marlow relaxed. The room was cloyingly warm enough to send anybody asleep, a definite sign that the elixir was working. Marlow shucked off her coat, throwing it over the sofa as she looked around for the drinks cabinet. She opened it and was disappointed to find it empty.

"Thirsty?"

"Mouth tastes like a sack of sawdust."

Dan picked up a thermos flask on the table and poured fresh coffee into one of several mugs sitting on a tray. "Here you go."

"I was hoping for something a little more potent," she said, taking the offered mug.

"Well, tough luck. You've had enough alcohol for one

lifetime."

Marlow took a sip of the bitter coffee. "Dad left you alone?"

"He went to bed. Left this just in case I needed it," He pointed to an antiquated TV in the corner of the room. It was so old the veneer on the wooden case was peeling and the curved grey cathode-ray tube screen was covered in dust. "I tried to get it to work, but it picks nothing up."

"I can't believe he left you alone!" snarled Marlow. "Typical irresponsible... what if something would've happened?"

Dan frowned. "Like what?"

"Like you channelling a horde into my dad's front room?"

"I didn't fall asleep. The elixir works."

It irritated Marlow that once again annoyed that her father was turning his back on problems without a thought of repercussions. "He didn't know that!"

"Of course he did, why would he leave me alone?"

Marlow drank the last of the coffee and slammed the cup down on the tray so hard the other mugs jumped. "Because that's what he does! He's irresponsible!"

Dan scowled, he clearly didn't agree. "Do you know that's your problem? You don't trust him. You don't trust anyone. And you give nobody else a break. It's always," his voice switched to a high-pitched mocking impersonation, "poor me, everybody in the world's got it in for Marlow, boo-hoo.'"

Marlow's wanted to raise her voice, shout back, and point out how wrong he was; how he was a just a kid who didn't understand the complexities of adult life. How Carlos had been the world's worst father and bullied her with relentless training... things he couldn't comprehend after living such a pamper life.

Dan turned away and stared at the blank television as he continued his rant. "So your dad threw you in front of monsters when you were a kid? How terrible. My dad left us. You know what he prepared me for? *Nothing.* Absolutely nothing at all."

Marlow's anger evaporated when she noticed tears rolling down Dan's cheek.

"Nothing," echoed Dan. He took a deep breath. "But you... your dad knew what he was doing. He knew you were the only one who could save the rest of us. Maybe you were too young to understand that? He prepared you for everything life had to throw at you, and all you did was complain and moan and ruin everything - even with your own family."

Marlow stamped her foot, raising her voice, refuting everything Dan had said - or at least she did in her head. In reality she sat mutely as the kid's accusations hit home.

"I bet your own kids think about you in exactly the same way you think of your own dad." He emphasised the words with a scathing inflection, "*exactly* the same." Dan moved to the window, wiping the condensation from the glass as he stared out. "I always wondered why my dad didn't even bother phoning me. I thought maybe he didn't have a phone, maybe something was holding him back... stupid excuses. Then I met you and I finally realised the truth." Marlow chose the wrong time to meet Dan's accusing gaze. "I realised that he could've called me any time, but he didn't care. He was a loser. Just like you."

Marlow tried to line up a perfect rebuttal. There was no way she was going to let some brat tear her apart - but the words refused to align into a coherent sentence.

Dan gazed back out of the window. "It's getting lighter. I'm going to get some breakfast."

He left the room. Marlow stared at the crackling flames and couldn't shake the feeling that she had just been emotionally ambushed.

CHAPTER THIRTEEN

A SULLEN SILENCE greeted Carlos as he entered the kitchen. Dan was shovelling a muesli swamp around his bowl, occasionally taking slow gulps of orange juice. Years of energy drinks and caffeine had fried his taste buds and he seldom drank anything else, so the juice was a rare luxury.

Marlow was hunched over the opposite side of the table, a coffee mug in one hand as she marked a pen across the map.

"Morning all," Carlos said cheerfully. He smiled at Dan. "So it worked, eh?"

"I feel terrific," exclaimed Dan with a relaxing sigh. "Like I've slept for a thousand years and don't need to anymore. I don't feel at all tired."

"Good, good." Carlos poured a coffee from the pot. His eyes darted to Marlow but neither appeared to want to continue the conversation.

Marlow circled her hometown and tapped Dan's house irritably. "I can't find any correlation!" Carlos looked over his daughter's shoulder, scanning the ink blots she had marked out. It followed their path across the country. "I thought there might be a geographic coloration. That the Infiltrators came through closer to Dan's home or had a better Conduit connection across ley lines. Something. Anything... but everything is centred around him." She jabbed the pen towards Dan.

"Well, at least he's not asleep now, is he?" said Carlos cheerfully.

"That doesn't solve our problem."

Carlos traced a finger over the map, coming to rest on Dan's neighbourhood. "It's there's no surprise you live there, Dan."

Dan looked between Carlos and the map. His hometown was nothing if not remarkable. "Why?"

Carlos took a seat alongside Marlow and regarded her with a certain amount of curiosity. "Why do you think we originally settled there?"

Marlow shrugged. "'Cause it was the furthest point from anything interesting?"

Carlos laughed, genuinely amused by her negativity. "Quite the opposite! Because for the likes us, it was prime real estate! It had a statistically higher Infiltrator average than anywhere else in the country. In the world, in fact. That's why, when you were fully trained and I retired, I got the hell out of there."

Marlow studied the map, willing an answer to reveal itself. "But I can't see any geographic cause..."

Carlos waved his hand dismissively. "There's probably one, but it's the people. I always suspected that, like us Hunters, some people are born Conduits. They just couldn't help it. They are just easier for the Infiltrators to use, just like some folks are more susceptible to hypnotism." Carlos's face clouded over as troubling memories took hold. "And that's where I first saw it."

Marlow and Dan exchanged their first curious glance of the morning.

"Saw what?" Dan asked in almost a whisper.

"The Darkmare."

Marlow grunted, a blend of disbelief and mocking humour. "That's just a fairy tale, dad."

Carlos jumped to his feet, suddenly full of nervous energy. "Not at all. No, no, no! Look..."

He darted from the room, leaving Dan and Marlow to lapse into awkward silence again. He reappeared moments later with a large leather-bound tome. At first Marlow thought it was the Book of Nightmares, but noticed it was slimmer and wider. She had never seen it before, which was odd as her father had sworn he'd handed everything across when he'd retired.

"This is my personal hunting journal." Carlos reverently laid the tome on the table and creaked open the first page. The pages were full of intricate illustrations: *Nightmarus Odonturus, Terrorium Extremus, Draco-marium,* the names were as familiar to Marlow as their grotesque images. He'd faced them all. Carlos turned the pages, finally stopping on a huge drawing that spilled across both pages. At first it looked like a mass of overlapping images before the brain finally broke the picture apart into its component images, like an illusion unravelling itself. "The Darkmare."

The Darkmare was a bulbous mass of flesh with a terrifying vertical slit of a mouth; tentacles and deformed limbs poked from the slimy mass. The overlapping images were other Nightmares breaking from blisters across the Darkmare's skin as it gave birth to the evil spawn.

"Looks like you were drunk when you drew this," Marlow quipped.

Dan went rigid. "I've seen that before!"

Carlos frowned. "Where?"

Dan scrutinized the picture, waiting for his memory to

play catch up. Extreme fatigue had all but shredded it; but now he remembered.

"I had a Nightmare back at the diner. It was the first nightmare I remember having... and I saw this. It was huge."

Carlos nodded. "The Darkmare is the source of all these... things. It's trying to push through from its own dimension into ours. It thirsts for our world, the warmth, the food... think of the Infiltrators you have encountered so far as nothing more than foot soldiers. Expendable and endless. The Darkmare wants to invade."

"This is just a myth," Marlow insisted. "and one you made up."

"Apparently nobody told *it* that it was a myth," said Carlos, taking his seat. "Hunters throughout the ages have suspected its existence. But I saw it, Marl. I saw the fabric of our realities split open and this is what lay beyond. This... aberration rules Innerspace. As soon as I saw it, I knew I was too old to face it. That's when I realised that I had to hand over the baton. Give up the one thing I enjoyed doing the most: hunting. The Darkmare had to be faced, eventually." Carlos slowly ran a hand down his wrinkled face. "It's a heart-wrenching feeling to realise you are too old; that the best days you had lay behind." He looked earnestly at Marlow. "That's why I wanted you to take over. To do all those incredible things I could not."

"What if I didn't wanna?" Marlow protested.

"The Darkmare must be stopped. For the sake of all humanity. If not you, then your heir. Your children... but you screwed that up."

Before Marlow could argue, Dan intervened.

"How come you saw it?"

"Because there was a Conduit. One with excessive power. Unheard of..." Carlos wagged a finger at Dan. "Until I met you, of course.". He nodded to Marlow, "Do you remember your Grandpa Adrian?"

Marlow nodded. "Think so. Bit Fat. Smelt of junk food."

Carlos smiled. "My father, yes. He was a legendary Hunter, and this was back in the day when you only had wit and skill to rely on. He was training me up, like I did with you - remember? When you whined about me destroying your childhood instead of thanking me for helping you prepare for life ahead?" Carlos waved his hand, dismissing any argument before it could manifest. "He was dealing with this young lad, this mighty Conduit. But instead of channelling through the usual Mares, when he fell asleep he broke the fabric of reality. Smashing between worlds as clear as if you tapped a window with a hammer, providing perfect access to the realm beyond." He tapped the page, "And that's when we saw what was beyond, manipulating the Conduit to push its way through. I stared death - true death - in the eyes. Oh, it had so many eyes," breathed Carlos in a trembling voice. He shook the memory away. "My father explained, or rather, gave me his theories, that the Darkmare was the source of this evil."

Dan's voice came as nothing more than a whisper. "Did you kill it?"

"It was beyond our skill. Besides, humans can't pass through the physical boundaries between worlds without being torn apart. Only strong Conduits can Astral Walk on the other side while they sleep. For them, it is just another dream where they can see and create whatever they desire. But for us mere mortals unable to project," he pointed to himself and Marlow, "it's a place we can never reach. Fortunately, we roused the lad awake and the portal sealed itself. He was not quite powerful enough a Conduit for the Darkmare to keep him under. Although if it had been you..." Carlos shivered at the thought.

Dan gazed at the map, imaging events in his mind's eye. He

had seen the Darkmare and experienced the same terror Carlos had.

"What happened to the lad?"

"Oh, we cured him. My father was a pioneering herbalist. He deduced that if the boy could sleep in a lighter state, avoiding the deeper REM stages, then he would be useless for the Darkmare's purposes."

"Could you do that for me? If I didn't sleep so deeply, maybe the monsters wouldn't come through."

He looked expectantly at Carlos when he received no answer. The doubtful expression on the old man's face spoke volumes.

"From what Marlow described, I'm not sure. You enter that deep sleep almost instantly. I'm not sure we could intercept the processes in time. Some things just can't be cured; you've just have to live with them."

"How old?" Marlow suddenly asked.

Carlos blinked several times as his thought process was derailed. "Pardon?"

Marlow was fixated on the map. "How old were you when this happened?"

"Twelve. About Dan's age; isn't that right?"

Marlow felt agitated, struck by a terrible thought. "And the lad was about the same. What was his name?"

Carlos shrugged. "I can't remember. It was so long ago and I must say the Darkmare occupied most of my thoughts back then."

"Didn't Grandpa keep records?"

"Of course he kept a ledger. It was a business after all." Carlos turned to the back of the tome where the final wad of pages contained a detailed list of jobs carried out, written in his father's meticulous hand. Carlos ran a finger down a column of figures. "I don't remember the exact date, but I do know it was a well-paid job. With everything that had happened, father upped his fees - ah, here we are."

Marlow read the name under her father's tapping finger. She felt a chill down her spine. "Oh my God..."

Dan craned to see. "What is it?" Then he saw the name: Boris Glass. "Same as me..."

"Your Grandpa," hissed Marlow.

"Don't be stupid..." but Dan knew it couldn't be a coincidence.

"You inherited your Grandpa's abilities," exclaimed Carlos. "That's why you're so powerful."

"Is that why I dreamt of the Darkmare?"

Marlow clenched her fists. "He knew! Your bloody grandpa damn well knew, and he didn't want to tell me." She was now shaking with a rage and stood to pace the kitchen. "That's why he contacted me. I should've wondered why he questioned nothing. *Anything*. It felt all so normal to him."

Dan shook his head. "Why would he do that?"

"The same reason he put you in that hotel the night after I vanquished the second Infiltrator. He knew there was a good chance another would come, so he stashed you away. Knew you'd inherited the ability but didn't wanna tell your mother about his dark little family secret! He didn't even speak up when she thought I'd kidnapped you. Oh no, that would be too much of a disgrace, right? Too late to admit anything!" Marlow boiled with rage.

Dan could scarcely believe it, although everything she was saying made perfect sense. "So... so he dumped me off with you?"

"Hoping I could find a cure without revealing what had happened in the past. He set me up!"

Dan didn't know what to say. He wanted to refute the accu-

sations. He wanted to tell Marlow that she was just being para-
noid - but it sounded authentic.

"So this is it? Because I have some family curse I'll have to
live on the run forever?"

"I think it may be so," sighed Carlos.

"NO!" Marlow snapped. "That ain't gonna happen!"

Both Dan and Carlos looked at her in surprise. Marlow
stabbed a finger at the map.

"We're going back. We're gonna find your Grandpa and end
this for good."

"How?" said Dan, fearing the answer.

"You're more powerful than your gramps, and he was able
to physically crack open a gap to both worlds." Marlow looked
to Carlos. "He can do that again?"

Carlos was thoughtful. "Presumably. The ability to Channel
doesn't appear to decrease with age. It's only whatever herbal
remedies my father gave him to repress the gift that would
prevent him from doing so."

"So we stop his meds, get him to open the portal and you
bring the Darkmare over." Marlow cracked her knuckles. She
was feeling energised from the revelation, despite her volcanic
anger towards Boris Glass. She had been set-up, used and
framed.

Now it was time to stop the madness.

It was time for revenge.

"Then I'm gonna blow his gloopy mass outta both
realities."

IT WAS JUST after eleven in the morning, and Dan was
surprised to be still alert. He wasn't sure if it was his imagination, but he could have sworn the colours around him were

more vivid and the new dusting of falling snow sparkled in the morning light.

Marlow and Carlos had plotted for most of the morning, which inevitably turned into an argument.

"No Dad, it's too dangerous!"

"I have to come, Marl! This is bigger than anything you have faced before."

Dan had pressed his eye close to the partially open kitchen door and seen Marlow leaned on the table, towering over her father with a raised finger.

"See? That's exactly your problem! You never believed I could do anything!"

"That's not true…" Carlos's voice faltered.

Marlow slumped. She rubbed her tired eyes and crumpled into the seat opposite. Dan wasn't sure if it was fatigue or the emotional toll of the argument. "You stole my childhood, Dad. Used it to turn me into a version of yourself you were never happy with."

"I was." Carlos reached across the table and squeezed his daughter's hand. "I was always impressed with you. You were a better Hunter than I ever was. You excelled…"

"You never said that."

The two of them looked at each other across the table. The air heavy with unspoken regret. Carlos was the first to find his voice again.

"I was afraid. To see your daughter become everything you could never be… and when your mother passed…" He sucked in a deep breath before he could continue. "I immersed myself in work. Hunting was the only occupation I had to keep my mind off this world."

"And me and my sis?"

"Your sister coped admirably," Carlos said with a slightly admonishing tone.

Marlow nodded, apparently no longer willing to argue. "Still doesn't change the fact that it's too dangerous for you to come, Dad. You're not what you used to be."

Carlos pulled back his hand and steepled his fingers. After a thoughtful pause he nodded solemnly, and the disagreement had dissolved into awkward unspoken feelings.

Carlos offered his car, pointing out that they wouldn't get much further in a stolen vehicle. Marlow loaded the Ford Estate with canvas bags and boxes she and Carlos had taken from the basement. Aside from practical conversation, nothing much further had passed between the two. Dan extended his arms and turned his face to the sky, snow blurring his glasses. He enjoyed the feeling of the flakes melting on his face; the soft sting from the cold. It was something he hadn't had a chance to do for so long. To pause and enjoy being alive.

Marlow slammed the boot closed and sighed as she regarded her father standing on the porch, hands thrust in his pockets to fight the cold. A look of envy and sadness etched on every crevasse of his face.

"You have the UV lamps?"

"Yes, dad."

"And the titanium cartridges?"

"You saw me load the box."

Carlos nodded absently. "And the neurotoxins for Boris..."

"All here, dad."

"Red topped ones, remember. They will sink him deep into a Conductive state, so be careful how you use them. What about the sandwiches?"

"Dad..."

Carlos cleared his throat, clearly wanting to say more than, "Good. Well. Remember the plan. Be safe."

Dan swore Marlow blushed. She bashfully kicked into the snow with the tip of her boots to avoid eye contact.

"Just one more thing," said Carlos, then disappeared briefly into the house, returning with a sheathed sword in the shape of a Samurai katana. "I want you to have this."

Marlow took it reverently. She'd trained with the sword as a child and remembered it being much bigger and heavier. Now it seemed small and fragile, although the craftmanship was more apparent than ever.

"I can't, dad. It's your most treasured possession."

"Not quite," said the old man. "There is your sister."

Marlow was about to snap back when she caught Carlos' mischievous look. Carlos tapped the sheath.

"This was forged from a meteor by your great-great-grandfather. It will slice through any Nightmare."

"Thanks." Marlow couldn't think of anything more meaningful to say.

Carlos pulled something from his pocket. "Oh, Daniel. Don't forget this." He tossed a small white-capped glass vial to him. At the last second, Dan caught the container inches before smashing on the ground. Although still sluggish, his reactions were improved. "More wake-up juice. The moment you feel tired, take half. Can't have you falling asleep now, can we?"

"Thank you, Mister Cornelius. Thanks for everything you've done for me."

A rare smile crossed the old man's face. Then he turned to Marlow and the smile faltered into something more neutral.

"Watch your backs."

Marlow opened the car door and hesitated. She rested her elbow on the roof, rubbed her bloodshot eyes, then forced herself to look at Carlos.

"Thanks, dad. Thanks for everything. I... I couldn't have done it without you. Any of it."

Dan saw the tear in the corner of Carlos's eyes, but it was swiftly swept aside as he pretended to adjust his glasses.

"I know. And you were wrong." Carlos wagged an admonishing finger. "I was always impressed. It's just difficult to accept the student can outgrow the master. Especially when she's your own flesh and blood. I'm proud of you, Marl." Now it was Marlow's turn to feign wiping snow from her eye. "Maybe after this... you might pop by for Christmas?"

Marlow's face twisted - and it took a moment for Dan to realise it was a smile - a genuine smile, not a smirk or a grin.

"Only if we get Gina to cook. You were always a terrible cook."

They climbed in the car, and Marlow gunned the engine. She glanced in the rear-view and gripped the wheel thoughtfully, then she became aware that Dan was staring. He opened his mouth to speak, but Marlow revved the engine to drown him out.

"Shut up, kid."

Without a further word or gesture, Marlow pulled away from the house. Dan lowered the side window, admitting a blast of cold air into the car, and waved goodbye until they turned a bend in the drive and lost sight of Carlos, who held his hand raised in a silent farewell the whole time.

"How you feeling?"

"Mmmm?"

"You ain't falling asleep on me now, are ya?"

Dan had been staring out of the window for a couple of hours as they drove through the increasingly heavy snow. Marlow had stayed off the major roads so as a result the car had skidded a few times, but she had always managed to keep them on the road.

"Where are we?" said Dan with a yawn.

"You just yawned," snapped Marlow.

"I know I did. I'm bored, not tired." That wasn't strictly true. While he wasn't feeling the familiar warm narcoleptic embrace, he was still weary and for the first time in his life he understood why people insisted on power naps. He thought it best not at alarm Marlow. "So where are we?"

"About five hours from home. I'm gonna have to pull over and take a nap. You, on the other hand, will have to stay awake and keep watch. Closer to home we're gonna have a tough time of avoiding the law so need to be on peak performance."

"I'm hungry," said Dan as his stomach rumbled. It was the only thing he could think to say.

THEY PARKED in a rest stop and ate the dry sandwiches Carlos had provided. Marlow reclined her seat to get comfortable, and Dan promised to stay awake and ensure the car didn't get snowed in.

Every time Marlow turned to get comfortable, the car rocked, but that was preferable to her long honking snores. Dan watched the hypnotic snowfall. He was starting to relax; unfolding into...

He shook himself. No! He couldn't risk falling asleep. He searched for the button to lower the window before finally realising it was done with an old crank handle. Just cranking it open an inch was enough to admit stabbing icy winds that blew snow into the car. It pricked his senses awake, but not enough to take away the underlying drowsiness he was experiencing. Dan pulled the white-capped vial of wake-up juice from his pocket and held it up to the low light coming through the windscreen. He could take a shot now, but he was certain he'd need the kick later. He took out his mobile and powered it up.

Marlow snorted, pulling her coat tighter around her neck. "Damn cold," she muttered.

"It was getting a bit stuffy in here." Dan expected her to wake in a panic to make sure he wasn't drifting off. She mumbled something incoherent, then lapsed into silence. Dan wasn't sure if she was asleep or not. "I would've thought you taken the chance to shower at your Dad's."

"Nice to see you patch things up with your Dad." Silence. Dan sighed and played with his phone for a moment. "Pity you couldn't be bothered doing the same with your own children." He continued flicking through his collection of games before realising that Marlow was staring at him. She hadn't moved position, but the faint light from the phone made her eyes gleam, reminding him of a cat. "What?"

"What would you say?" she asked.

"To your children? How about sorry for being a crappy mum. Sorry for being too scared to pick up the phone and talk to you. Maybe a little about how they meant the world to you and how you'll make up all that lost time." The words had come out in a pent-up rush, and Dan had to catch his breath. "That's what I'd want to hear my dad say." Dan sensed Marlow's gaze bore into him but refused to meet it. Talking was one thing, but he had no energy for an argument. She suddenly snatched the phone from him. "Hey! What're you doing?"

Marlow's finger hovered over the screen. Dan could see the indecision play across her face. He held his breath, surprised she was even considering doing the right thing, and willed her to make the call.

With a hiss, Marlow chucked the phone back into Dan's lap.

"What's the point? It's too late now."

Dan offered the phone to her. "This could be your last chance."

Marlow lowered her seat, resigned to losing the battle with sleep. "What d'you mean?"

"I thought it was obvious. Me and you driving into battle against the Darkmare. Tearing a hole between worlds just so you can blow it away. You act like there's no danger involved."

"Nothing I can't handle."

"Rubbish. You could die doing this. Look at you. You've been beaten up pretty badly already by just a couple of Infiltrators, now you expect to effortlessly stop them all? And what about me?"

"Conduits are always safe."

"What if the Darkmare decides that I'm more hassle than I'm worth? What if it decides to kill me and start all over?" Marlow's jaw clenched, she'd obviously hoped Dan wouldn't be aware of the danger. "Or worse. You fail completely and the Darkmare breaks through. Then I'd be trapped in a permanent vegetative state. I'd never wake up, would I? Just grow old and slowly starve as it runs riot, killing mum, grandpa, you - everybody I care about!" Marlow blinked in surprise - but Dan steamrolled on. "It's time you grew up and realised that not everybody else you is like you! You can't drown all your problems in a bottle and you can't choose to ignore people who might actually want to be around you!" Dan's temper flared. He let it out, the only thing now keeping him awake. "Did you give even a second's thought to how I might feel about you using my grandpa to fight this thing?"

"He—"

"You're using him as bait! I don't care that he was trying to hide all this from mum. I know he was doing it because he cared! I know he made a mistake, and if he is the only one who can help us, then he'll have to whether he likes it or not. And that hurts! That makes me feel like I'm betraying him!"

"He used us! Why should you care? He never told you the truth."

"Which is exactly why I see we have to do what we have to do. That's what I'm saying - sometimes you have to take the toughest option to do the right thing. It's about time you did that too." He folded his arms. A clear signal that the conversation was not only over, but any further words would just be a waste of oxygen.

"Maybe we should run the engine a bit. Warm us up," Marlow said in a dry croak. It took a few turns of the key to spark the engine to life. The air conditioner came straight on, full blast, blowing frigid air at them. Once ticking over it took several minutes for the vehicle to warm up. Marlow made use of that time to get out and clear the accumulated snow from the windows and clear the wheels. When she got back in, Dan spoke as if nothing had passed between them.

"Are you awake enough to drive?"

"I'm awake enough to kick the world into shape. Thanks for your concern." The last seeped with sarcasm.

Dan considered it a personal triumph that he stayed awake for the rest of the journey. The cold air and locking onto the loudest rock stations had occupied him while Marlow bore the distractions in sullen silence. The snow had kept most traffic off the roads, particularly police patrols, so it was with a tremendous sense of relief that Dan saw a signpost showing home lay ahead.

This was it. Full circle to face down his own personal nightmares. He only hoped that Marlow knew what she was doing.

CHAPTER FOURTEEN

MARLOW DIDN'T KNOW what she was doing.

She had become increasingly anxious as they approached the town. The traffic had naturally increased despite the late hour and constant snow. One police car had passed them, but the lack of any sudden high-speed pursuit had boosted their confidence, but did little to calm Marlow's frayed nerves.

Towering metal poles decorated with jolly Christmas illuminations and topped with a compliment of surveillance cameras became more frequent. Marlow prayed the snow would provide enough cover against a vigilant operator consulting the Most Wanted list. Added to that was the ever-present and increasing fear that Dan would fall asleep. As far as she could tell the kid had been awake for twenty-four hours. She knew most people couldn't last much longer without sleep, and that terrified her more than she liked to admit.

With each passing moment her desire to ditch the vehicle increased until she finally pulled over in a bland housing estate, each building looking like a clone of the other. The occasional

house was decked with colourful illuminations that blazed
pointlessly throughout the night.

"What're we doing here?" Dan asked. "This isn't anywhere
near where I live."

"Close enough," Marlow cut the engine. "We walk from
here. You'll just have to carry a few things."

The few things weighed Dan down as his feet slipped in
snow that came above his ankles and seeped into his trainers,
making his feet wet and cold. Marlow had opened the cases in
the car, revealing an arsenal of gleaming weapons; obviously
not belonging to her, as they were well-maintained and
gleamed in the yellow streetlights. The thrill of shouldering
several high-powered rifles soon vanished when she added a
backpack filled with ammunition and strapped her chipped
baseball bat to that.

Marlow was similarly laden with equipment, including her
trusty blunderbuss, but further scrutiny was denied when
Marlow wrapped a cloak around her and then fastened one
around Dan. Less to keep out the cold and more to artfully
disguise the fact they were carrying an enormous amount of
illegal firepower.

Marlow's hands shook as she tied Dan's cloak. She'd always
felt frightened facing Infiltrators, no matter how many times
she'd done it, which is why she preferred to stagger into battle
drunk. Now she was not only sober, but responsible for the
kid's safety as they faced down the very beast she had sneered
at her father for believing in.

If that were not nerve jangling enough, there was a further
complication, a feeling that was alien to Marlow. It had taken
her most of the drive to identify it: the intangible honour in
fulfilling her family obligation. The look in her father's eyes
had conveyed more words than he'd ever spoke to her. They

were wide with pride, wide with love, and wide with the certain knowledge he wouldn't see his daughter alive again.

As they tramped through the snow towards Dan's home, she shooed the negative thoughts aside. There was no room for them tonight. She would survive this. She was determined to protect Dan and, just as importantly, prove her father wrong. That alone was worth living for.

Letting Dan take the lead, they kept to the darkest streets, thankful there was nobody around. A few vehicles had passed, mostly taxis, so they both lurked in the shadows until the coast was clear. It wasn't until they were several streets away did Dan speak up.

"What are we going to tell grandpa?"

Marlow didn't have a clue. She knew the moment the door opened that the kid's mother or Boris would be racing to the phone to call the cops. She'd have to stop them as painlessly as possible.

"Dunno," she finally admitted. "You ain't feeling tired, are ya?"

"The cold's doing a good job at keeping me perky."

That sounded evasive, but she didn't pursue it. Dan suddenly stopped on a corner.

"What's wrong?" Marlow looked around suspiciously.

"We turn onto my street here." Dan peeked around the corner - and quickly pulled his head back. "Uh-oh."

Marlow peered around the corner and immediately saw the problem. A police car was parked outside, no doubt waiting for the wily kidnapper to make contact and demand her ransom. This was a problem she hadn't expected.

"Crap," she growled. "Now what?"

Dan cleared the slush from his glasses. "I have an idea."

Marlow listened. With each sentence, she felt increasingly uncertain. The plan Marlow had concocted with her father lacked several vitally important details, especially in execution and how to get out alive. However, they had not discussed how to deal with unwelcome human interference. Dan's plan was rough, full of potential pitfalls, and so clearly improvised that if it was analysed for more than a few seconds, it fell apart. Sadly, it was the only option they had.

When Marlow finally nodded her consent, Dan looked awkwardly away and spoke so low that Marlow could barely hear.

"Just so you know... whatever happens. Thank you."

Marlow was shocked. Nobody *ever* said thank you. They were often so relieved that the hideous creature which had trampled through their house was destroyed that they threw the cash at her on the doorstep in their haste to get rid of her, as if it was Marlow's fault the Infiltrator had appeared.

Marlow flinched when Dan reached out and awkwardly patted her on the arm. "You've been a friend. A real friend who stood by me when... well, when things went crazy and nobody else would. I'd hug you... but you stink." He handed her his phone. "While you're waiting. It's got enough credit on it. Good luck."

Dan dumped his equipment in Marlow's arms, only making sure he had the wake-up juice and neurotoxins hidden in his pocket. Then headed to his home, a dark spot devoid of any festive sheer. Unaccustomed to meaningful human contact, Marlow stood in shock, wondering what had just happened. It was only when Dan was halfway to his house did she duck into the shadows of a side street and lost herself in the park.

WHEN THE FRONT DOOR OPENED, Dan *fleetly* glimpsed his mother's face. Her mouth wide open and tears streaming down her cheeks as she engulfed him in a hug that crushed the

breath from him. With his face nestled against her, he could
smell nothing but the familiar warm and soothing scent of
home. He couldn't hear a word she was saying because her arm
covered his ears, but he caught the gist of it.

"I'm OK, mum. Completely fine!"

He pulled away so he could breathe and noticed he was
being carefully studied by a frowning Police Woman - who was
then nudged aside by his grandpa who embraced him even
harder.

"I thought we'd lost you, son," Boris sobbed.

Dan's thoughts were in turmoil. If grandpa was so regretful
then why didn't he say anything about his own nightmare-ish
past? If he'd known so much, why hadn't he tried to help
earlier? Now he was home, Dan was beginning to have doubts.
Had Carlos and Marlow been correct in identifying his grand-
father as the kid who once mastered opening a rift between
worlds? It had been a long time ago. From Boris's reaction, he
now doubted it.

Before he knew what was happening, he was whisked into
the living room and onto the couch. Everybody spoke at once,
including the Police Woman. He didn't know who to reply to
first. What he wanted was to sleep, and the sudden attention
was overpowering. Drowsiness hit him like a sledgehammer.
Relief at being at home. The familiar environment was too
much of a lull to resist. Carlos's brew was wearing off. His hand
went for his coat pocket - and he was surprised to see his coat
was missing. His mother must have pulled it off during the
melee. Recalling the details of the last few moments was like
scrambling in fog. Just the fleetest images. It was only when his
eyelids fluttered that Boris nudged him with a sharp elbow to
the ribs and urgently spoke up.

"He's tired. Let me put the coffee on." He dashed from the
room.

Dan fought to stay awake. All he needed a jolt of Carlos's elixir and he'd be fine for another twenty-four hours. His mother's arm was still firmly affixed around his shoulders, anchoring him to the sofa as she continued to sob. The Police Officer took Boris' place and smiled in a friendly manner.

"Hello, Daniel. My name is Officer Janet. How are you feeling?"

"Fine. Dan... hate Daniel..." He was finding it difficult to speak, his tongue felt thick as he yawned.

"You had us all worried when you went missing. The woman who was with you, where is she?"

His mother's musky scent and the overly warm room was sabotaging his efforts to stay awake. The room swam and his words became a drowsy whisper.

"'S OK. She's fine... I need my coat." He tried to stand, but his mother's vice-like grip held him in place.

"Where is she, Dan?"

Dan spoke but only a slurred mumble came out. He must concentrate. Marlow's life depended upon it.

Rhythmically flashing lights from the Christmas tree and the warm pulse from a ceramic snowman decoration lulled him. The room grew dim and the voices came from far away - but what did that matter if he was safe?

Safe enough to sleep...

Ssssleeeeepp.

The last came as a sibilant hiss cutting through his unconsciousness. He'd heard it before, many times. Now he was in the zone on the edge of consciousness, he could identify it as the voice that lulled him to sleep almost every hour of his life. The same voice that had seized his narcolepsy and used it as a tool for its own gain. He had never recalled it before, but now he knew it was the voice of the Darkmare. A voice he had heard his whole life. His oldest friend he was now discovering was his darkest enemy.

Ssssslllleeeepppp...

It wasn't a suggestion; it was a hostile command. Something that had ruined his life. Carlos's wake-up juice must still be trickling through his system as the transition between wakefulness and sleep was usually seamless.

"NO!" shouted Dan as loud as he could, commanding his muscles to act and jerk him awake. The smell of coffee punched through the drowsiness and he sat bolt upright, almost spilling the cup grandpa Boris hovered in front of his nose. "Marlow!"

"Yes," Officer Janet said, squeezing his hand, completely misinterpreting the situation, "Marlow Cornelius. Where is she?"

Dan struggled against the warm tendrils of drowsiness trying to pull him back into the comfy sofa. He swore he could feel them, as sticky as treacle, massaging the stress from his shoulders and back, subliminally assuring him that everything was OK and he should just relax...

He snatched the coffee. It spilled over the rim and scalded his cold legs. His throat was accustomed to drinking nuclear-hot liquids, and he swallowed it all in three gulps. However, he was far beyond the effects of caffeine and it delivered only a tiny jolt.

"My coat!" he barked between coughs from drinking too quickly.

"Tell us about Marlow," urged Janet.

"I need my coat!" Dan insisted.

Confused by his outburst, his mother burst into a fresh sobbing and rubbed his arm, "Ssshh, I've hung it up. You don't need it now."

Her very touch was making him relax. He shucked her off

and tried to stand, but his legs had decided to sleep even if the rest of him hadn't. He wobbled and collapsed on the floor - his head narrowly missing cracking against the coffee table that grandpa had hastily nailed back together.

"What's wrong with him?" screamed his mother. "What has she done to him?"

"Need... my... coat..." hissed Dan as he shook his head to stay awake. From the helpless looks around him, he knew it must look like he was having a fit as he writhed on the carpet. He reached for grandpa, who took an involuntary step back. "Wake-up juice..."

Even in his rehabilitated state he saw grandpa become rigid, his face paling.

Then everybody was suddenly speaking.

"What's happening?"

"I'll call a paramedic!"

"He's having a seizure!"

"Coat..." muttered Dan.

Boris darted into the hall and rapidly searched Dan's coat pockets. His fingers found a small glass cylinder, and he returned.

"Got it!" said Boris as he wrestled with the cap.

Dan's vision began to grey. Desperate, he tried to sit up, but his arms felt like jelly and his legs were numb.

"Wake... up..."

"Take this," said Boris urgently.

Dan felt the glass vial pushed to his lips, and he drank the liquid. Instead of the sharp jolt he expected, the voices became unintelligible, and he swore he could hear a bell.

He caught sight of the open vial in Boris's hand, and the red bottle cap in the other. Red. He had drank the neurotoxins designed to knock Boris out so he could open the fracture between realms.

The last thought to carousel through his mind was how he'd let Marlow down in his own plan. The toxin had such a powerful torporific effect that he instantly fell into a catatonic sleep.

"PIZZA?"

It was such an uninspiring thing to say, so not surprisingly it was the first idea that popped into Marlow's head. When Dan outlined his plan it had made perfect sense, although, in retrospect, it could have done with another hour or two of brainstorming as it left several key details blank.

Dan was to enter the house first and distract everybody, allowing Marlow to stealthily break in, thus surprising everybody and taking control of the situation so things could be explained without her being carted away by the cops. All perfectly achievable.

Marlow had circled through the park that ran behind Dan's house. The darkness, snow covered potholes and ditches, and the weight of the weaponry she carried had made it almost impossible.

Ditching most of the weaponry in the hedges at the perimeter of Dan's back garden, Marlow sneaked up to the back door, which was always kept open when the family was home.

It was locked.

She had cursed under her breath as she futilely tugged at the handle. No doubt the cops secured the house, a problem she should have anticipated - *would have* anticipated if she wasn't feeling so worn out.

Every window was shut to both the night chill and any prowling intruders. Marlow circled around to the front of the house, checking the coast was clear from any law enforcement that happened to be watching and crept up to the front door. She heard raised voices inside, and shadows cast against the curtains revealed there was a problem. She'd have to act fast - and the only idea that occurred to her was inspired by a rumbling stomach.

She rang the bell.

Boris Glass eventually answered the door, clutching Dan's coat. His eyes widened in instant recognition when he saw Marlow.

"Pizza?" repeated Marlow in a foolhardy hope it would trick the old man into keeping the door open.

Boris thrust the door closed. Marlow slid her foot in the gap, the heavy wood crushing her boot. She shouldered the door open and swung the blunderbuss under Boris's chin. She didn't have time for niceties. Boris raised is hands, dropping the coat.

Marlow shoved her way into the house. Marlow trampled over Dan's coat as she entered the hallway, kicking the front door closed behind. She marched a terrified Boris straight into the living room.

Bryony Glass was kneeling over her son, gently tapping his cheek and urgently uttering: "Wake up, Dan! For heaven's sake, wake up!"

Marlow saw her gaze wasn't on Dan, but on the shadows slowly swelling in the corner of the ceiling. The Police Woman hadn't yet noticed and reacted the moment she recognized Marlow striding in with a weapon. She leapt to her feet - calculating whether she had time to disarm the intruder without endangering anybody. It took a split second for her to decide it was impossible. She raised her arms in a placating manner.

"Put the gun down, Marlow. The boy's having a seizure and there are more officers outside."

Marlow ignored her. "It's not a seizure. Wake him up!"

"I'm trying!" Bryony squealed. "What have you done to him?"

"What've I...? Hell, ask your Pop about that one. He's the one covering all this up."

Bryony's gaze slipped to Boris, who stepped away from the business end of the gun. The guilt on his face was evidence enough.

Marlow knelt next to Dan. "What d'you give him?" Then she saw the empty red-capped vial on the table. "Oh no... tell me you didn't!"

"He asked for it!" snapped Boris.

"No! That was for you... damn it! He needs the wake-up juice. The one with the white cap! Where's his coat?" Out of the corner of her eye she saw the Police Woman tense, ready to spring. Marlow didn't bother looking up, but waved the blunderbuss in warning. "Don't think about it."

Boris held up Dan's coat. "You mean this?"

The flicker of hope Marlow had been nurturing suddenly extinguished. Her own boot print was stamped over the pocket, from which a wet stain pushed through the fabric. Boris carefully turfed the pocket inside out, revealing crushed glass.

"Ah, crap..." wailed Marlow.

Then Bryony screamed in terror. Marlow felt as if Hunters of old possessed her as her fatigue ebbed and the lifelong instincts her father had drilled into her seized control. Instantly alert and in control.

With one hand she reached out and grabbed the Police Woman by the scruff of the neck. The cop screeched as Marlow pulled her aside. She hadn't seen the twisted shark head, the size of the coffee table, swim through the dense dark hole that had formed in the corner ceiling. Beyond the beast, Marlow could see a faint purple light playing on nightmarish mountain peaks. She had only a fleeting glimpse of the Dream-scape before the bulk of the creature blocked it as it attempted to haul itself out. The ferocious head snarled, dry skin pulled taut against slender opaque fangs. The head lunged forward, mounted on an implausibly long neck.

"Dream's over," growled Marlow as she raised the blunder-buss and pulled the trigger.

Both barrels clicked on empty chambers.

The beast butted Marlow squarely in the chest. Something crunched and excruciating pain rippled across through her side as a rib broke. She was plucked off her feet and hurled across the room, into the wall. Plaster crunched, and she fell hard on the floor.

The Infiltrator roared, its malevolent gaze on Marlow as it heaved its bulk from the portal. It didn't see Officer Janet snatched a small table from the side of the sofa and broke it across the fiend's head. Wood splintered, but it was enough to leave a nasty gash exposing blue crystalline flesh beneath. With a squeal, it diverted its attention to the other humans in the room.

Officer Janet and Bryony retreated to the corner of the room. The sight before them was beyond anything they could rationally comprehend. Primitive instinct instructed them not to scream, but to close their eyes and remain utterly silent in the hope the beast would vanish like all good nightmares did.

Except this one.

Jaws opened wide with a visceral scream – which was suddenly cut short as a sword blade stabbed through its jaw and up into its skull. Marlow twisted the blade as she retracted it, decapitating the monstrosity. The head fell, shattering on impact. The rest of the body twitched, then turned into blue ice, then imploded as the surrounding portal closed.

For a moment there was nothing but the sound of heavy

breathing and sobbing. Then Marlow pulled herself up, one hand clutching her broken rib, the other twirling the midnight katana blade in a lethal fluid gesture. She slid it back in the sheath on her back, then retrieved the blunderbuss.

"What the hell was...?" Officer Janet stammered as she struggled to maintain her sanity.

"*Carcharodon Nightmarus*," Marlow quoted as she fished ammo cartridges from her pocket and loaded the weapon. The pain in her chest was making it difficult to speak. "Try to wake Dan up."

Bryony nodded and scrambled on all fours to her son. Cartridges loaded, Marlow snapped the barrel in place and aimed at Boris. "You got something to tell me?"

"I do." Officer Janet was struggling to maintain her composure, but seeing Marlow had given her something real she could cling to. "Marlow Cornelius, you're under arrest."

Keeping the blunderbuss on Boris, Marlow slowly turned to face her with a look of pure defiance. "I don't think I'm gonna let you arrest me today."

The cop considered for a moment, then nodded and stepped back.

Marlow turned to face Boris and waved the gun in a threatening gesture. "So?"

"What do you want me to say?"

"Sorry for landing me in in the shit for one." She glanced at Officer Janet and indicated to Boris. "Did he bother to tell ya he hired me to look for the kid?" The cop shook her head. Marlow turned her back to Boris. "And I bet you never told your daughter about your own past, right? What you passed on to Dan?"

Bryony looked up from gently shaking Dan. "What's she talking about?"

Boris's eyes never left Marlow's as his hostility melted in to resignation. "I'll tell you later. Wake him up!"

"He's not coming around! What have you done to him?" she shrieked at Marlow.

"God's sake! Will everyone quit asking what have I done to the kid? I wasn't even in the room! I did nothing except save his butt! Old Boz here gave him a shot of something designed to knock him out," she pointed to Boris to clarify just who was supposed to be unconscious.

Boris dropped to his knees and felt for a pulse in Dan's neck. "He's in a deep sleep. Almost like a coma."

Marlow punched the air in helpless frustration. "*You* were supposed to take the neurotoxin, open up the rift to bring the Darkmare through so I could pop it and end all this."

"Excuse me," said Officer Janet cautiously stepping between them to get their attention. "Can somebody explain what is going on."

At that moment a great wail rose from outside. A hideous otherworldly roar that made every human who heard it tremble in unquestioning fear. It was immediately followed by the unmistakable wail that only a mass of panicking people can make. Then a deep rumbling, the sound of rending metal and a dozen car alarms suddenly shrieking in unison.

Marlow ran to the window. Cupping her hands against the glass, she peered out. When she turned back to the others, her expression was unreadable.

"What has happened?" Officer Janet asked firmly.

Marlow ran her fingers through her hair. "The end of the world by the looks of it."

CHAPTER FIFTEEN

ON THE FAR side of town, the sky had rent open as if made of glass. Through the broken shards of reality was a whole new world. Snow clouds had torn and the sky... or rather, the nether-sky, was like those Marlow had only ever peeked at before. A deep purple lit by some far-off alien sun, with swirling red aura clouds rotating like time-lapse footage.

But that's not what chilled Marlow.

A mass of crawling limbs and undefined shapes undulated through the crimson haze, heading for the bridge between worlds. The vanguard of unspeakable terrors pushed into the town. They were distorted, a heat haze between dimensions blissfully masking them. But push through they did.

Homes immediately opposite blocked the view, so Marlow couldn't see the damage caused, but the flicker of flames towering high into the night sky spoke volumes. The town was the battlefront.

Boris peered out, trembling. "*Dan* did this?"

Officer Janet pushed past and cupped her hands around her

eyes to see for herself. They all heard the faint gasp of aston-ishment from her.

"You were supposed to be the one. This is what you used to do, right? Well, it looks like Dan can do it much better than you."

Bryony's eyes narrowed as she looked between them, then focused on her father. "You knew all about these things? About Dan's... condition?"

"When I was younger..."

"My dad helped you so you thought I'd be able to help Dan. Why didn't you say anything? Was it because you were too embarrassed about what he'd inherited from you?"

"Yes," Boris backed slightly as the two women rounded on him. "I saw what had happened... but I knew something could be done about it."

"If you told me this from the beginning, then we wouldn't be here. Instead, you lied to Dan, lied to your own daughter. Lied to me and set me up with the cops to take the fall instead of telling the truth."

"Who'd believe me?"

Officer Janet finally staggered back from the window and took a moment to compose herself. "If somebody doesn't tell me what is occurring here, I'll have you all arrested for... for...."

"Shut up!" Marlow turned to Bryony and wagged the blun-derbuss at Boris. "He owes you and me a huge apology."

Boris knelt at Dan's side and gently caressed his hair. "I thought I could solve this... yes, I had the same issues as a child. I channelled nightmares, just as my father had done beforehand. It is a family curse."

"Wait, nightmares?" began Officer Janet, but nobody paid her attention.

Boris continued with a gesture to Bryony. "You were my only child and apparently my form of the ability is only inherited to the male family line, so it skipped a generation until you had Dan."

Bryony frowned as she processed the revelation. "Why did it stop happening to you?"

Marlow chimed in. "My grandpa gave him a remedy that stopped the Infiltrators from using him."

Boris nodded. "I secretly tried them on Dan, but they did nothing more than make his narcolepsy worse. He got *that* from your mother's side of the family," he added defensively, "I suppose it countered the remedy. That's when I knew I had to turn to professional help."

"But without the facts what could I do? Dan thought the only solution was to run away."

Officer Janet held up her hand to intervene and turned to Bryony. "Sorry, but does this make any sense to you?"

"Sadly, yes."

Marlow turned to the Officer. "You have nightmare, right?" The cop nodded. "Good, then all you gotta know is their realm is spilling onto our streets and that kid is the tap that's allowing them to do it. The plan was to get gramps here to open the portal so I could lure the Darkmare out and kill it."

"What the what?" stammered Officer Janet.

Marlow waved her hand dismissively. "Don't worry about it. Seems we were all wrong to think that Boris could ever be useful."

"I still can be."

"Oh yeah? What? A couple more guns are only useful up to a certain point."

"I have the answer that eluded your family. I spent my life looking into this. It was automatically assumed that my ability physically opened the tear between worlds."

Marlow shrugged. "Seems like Dan can do that all without ya. Talented kid."

"Which means whether it was me or him, the portal is now open for you to do what you need to do." Marlow blinked in surprise. That hadn't occurred to her. "But my point is, all this - it's not *him*. It wasn't even *me*. Granted, we channel the creatures better than anyone else can, but the *reason* they come through here more than anywhere isn't to do with our affliction. It's an environmental issue."

A faint explosion from outside sent Officer Janet running to the window again.

Marlow's attention was fixed on Boris. "Okay, just pretend I'm dumb…"

"That is very easily done. After my injury in the police force, I turned to civil engineering. Part of that involved a geological survey of land where permits were issued. I found a high quantity of quartz around here. A significant quantity in fact."

Officer Janet pulled away from the window. She was ashen. "Whatever's out there is heading this away! I think I just saw the shopping centre go up in flames."

"Quartz?" said Bryony. "How does this help any of us?"

"Quartz is used in speakers to amplify the sound," explained Boris. "Any form of energy waves in fact."

"My dad always thought the Infiltrators use waves, inter-dimensional frequencies we can't ordinarily detect, that travel between worlds, to fix onto a Conduit and create the connection between them."

"Exactly," said Boris. "The land beneath us, this entire region, is acting as a huge oscillator and magnifying the signal. Dan's abilities are being replicated a hundredfold - enough to open the portal." He shook his head sadly and rubbed the bridge of his nose. "Bringing him back was the worst thing you could have done."

Marlow wanted the ground to swallow her whole. She had

just played straight into the Darkmare's clutches. Was the beast really that cunning?

"So what d'we do?"

"I thought you would know the answer to that," said Boris bleakly.

Bryony cradled Dan's head, wiping the film of cold sweat off his forehead.

"You have to save my son, Miss Cornelius. Do whatever it takes, but you must save him."

Marlow fought against the smothering sense of despair and utter defeat. An unnatural smile crawled across her face but failed to reach her eyes.

"Sure. Not a problem."

MULTIPLE COLOURED auroral hues rippled across the sky as two worlds collided with such titanic force that the laws of nature were torn asunder. Purple lightning struck, hammering craters into the ground.

The portal slowly expanded, crumbling buildings caught in its path and dissolving the landscape like acid as it encompassed street after street. Creatures poured from the opening, all manner of shapes and twisted forms that could only originate in the darkest recesses of a fevered dream.

There was an exodus of people. Some took to their cars, which the more colossal creatures effortlessly chewed apart. Wrecking ball fists struck buildings, knocking them aside and flames from leaking gas mains formed geysers, setting neighbouring properties alight. The air was alive with clicks and harsh screeches that jarred primal nerves and formed pulsed of dread through the spine. The sibilant drone and high-pitched chittering of the invaders was an orchestra of madness.

Beyond the shimmering mist of the portal, *something*

colossal moved. An unseen intelligence on the edge of consciousness and sleep. From there it commanded events. This was only a small town, the first fracture into a reality whose warmth had attracted it for eons. But it knew even a minor fracture could grow to topple a mountain.

MARLOW AND BORIS hunkered down behind a white van, the front half of which had been partially crushed. They had spent that last ten minutes pushing towards the portal and evading Infiltrators. They had only passed a handful of people and the closer they got, the emptier the streets became.

Marlow had armed herself with the blunderbuss and a bandolier of exotic ammunition over her shoulder. The katana crossed her back and the reliable baseball bat hanging from her waist. Boris selected a sawn-off shotgun from the weapons cache Marlow had discarded in the garden, but felt uncomfortable wielding it. He had wanted to stay behind with his family, but Marlow had pressured him to come.

She didn't relish the man's company and loathed him for what he had put her and Dan through, but she suspected the old man's latent powers would still prove useful. Another factor was Marlow needed backup. She hadn't slept well for days and every time she closed her eyes she was convinced she'd fall sleep. That terrified her. What made it more frightening was the thought that her oneirism would send her into a timeless oblivion. A costly mistake that could lead to the end of the world. No short nap was worth that.

BEFORE LEAVING, Marlow had lain Dan on the sofa and had assured Bryony that they were safe to stay put. The Infiltrators needed Dan asleep, so they shouldn't attack the house. She

was in the safest place on the planet - although Marlow had
advised her to barricade the doors and windows after they had
left, just in case. Officer Janet had agreed to stay with her.

Staring at Dan, Marlow had felt an oddly fierce desire to do
anything to protect the kid. The last time she had ever experienced such an intense feeling was with her own children...

Would she ever see them again?

Probably not.

That revelation had struck her hard. *She would never see
them again. This was a suicide run.*

The idea had stubbornly taken root in her mind. If she
wasn't around to tell them, they would not understand how she
felt about them; her actions sure as hell didn't tell them. She
took Dan's mobile phone.

"Gotta make a call," she'd mumbled and hastily left the
room.

In the kitchen Marlow had made a pretence of checking
the other windows had been securely barricaded as she tried to
recall her old home number. Luckily Trebor still replied on the
old landline so it was unlikely to have changed. She dialled the
number, but hovered over the call button for several seconds
pondering who would answer? What would she say? What
would...

She thumbed the button, knowing it was the only way to
silence the nagging doubts. Her heart had skipped as it rang. It
was answered on the third ring by a quavering girl's voice.

"Yes?"

Marlow tried to speak, but only a wheeze hissed out.

"Hello?" the voice now sounded wary.

Marlow's jaw worked, but only guttural sounds emerged
past the ball of emotions choking her.

"I think it's one of them," said the voice, slightly more
distant as it spoke to somebody in the same room. Another

faint voice answered, "Hang up, honey!" Marlow had no problem in identifying Trebor's voice.

"No, wait!" Marlow had exclaimed in a rush of words. "It's me... it's your mum."

Silence.

Marlow wondered if the line had been disconnected, then heard shuffling from the other end.

"Molly, it's me, sweetheart. Your mum."

"Hi mummy." Molly's voice rose an octave with unmistakable delight. "Are you coming to save us?"

"What?"

"They're here, mummy, I—"

"Give me that! Marlow?" snapped Trebor. "You pick a hell of a time to call!"

"What's happening?"

"Look outside! You tell me. They're everywhere!"

Marlow had been so focused on the immediate problem that it hadn't occurred to her that the creatures outside had already spread to the suburbs. Placing her own children in jeopardy.

"They already got Mrs Hitchcock from next door and the Freemans were hiding out in the tree house when *something* ate it whole!"

"Calm down," Marlow had been amazed at the commanding tone of her own voice, as fear escalated Trebor's.

"I barricaded the downstairs windows and got the kids upstairs, but I can still see—"

"SHUT UP, TREBOR!" roared Marlow, years of repressed frustration coming to a boil. To her surprise, he had complied. "They're Infiltrators, Trebor. Nightmares. You know, the things you didn't think I should deal with..."

His reply was almost inaudible, "I know. Marlow... I'm... sorry. I was wrong. We... we need you."

At last, the long awaited apology. Marlow was surprised that it didn't fill her with the smugness and satisfaction she'd imagined. After waiting so long for it, it felt pointless.

"You did well heading upstairs. Make sure the chimney and the loft hatch is secure and get every room well lit. If they do come in hit them with everything you've got - right in the eyes."

"I already have. They shatter when–"

"Good. And whatever you do, don't go asleep. Don't let the kids sleep either. That's how these things can get in. Now the portal's open, I suspect they might be able to use *anyone*. Tell me you understand."

"Y-yes. Marlow, I'm so sorry. Sorry for everything. You were right..." Trebor was choking with emotion. "We're so scared. The kids... they need you here... I need..."

A loud boom from outside had gently shaken the building, reminding Marlow that time was running out. Every fibre of her being wanted to race to protect her children - but a rational part of her brain knew that would be an endless battle. The only way to stop this was at the source. Face the Darkmare.

Easier said than done.

"I have to go and stop this thing."

"How? That's impossible!"

"Impossible's what I do. Now put the kids on. I wanna speak to them."

Trebor handed the phone back to Molly, and she'd heard the sounds of bickering as she and Jamie wrestled the handset between them in their eagerness to speak.

"Mummy?' came their voices in unison. "Are you coming to help us?"

That was a knife in the heart. "Your dad's looking after you just fine. I am coming, but I just got to do something first. I'm gonna help *everyone*."

Jamie's voice had wavered. "The Darkmare?"

"You remember?" Marlow felt proud that they remembered the twisted stories she used to tell them.

"'Course. I miss our stories"

"Then you know what I'm gonna be doing. I'll see you straight after. Deal?"

"Deal!" they chorused.

"Love you guys. Don't forget that." Marlow's eyes tightly closed as she spoke, her knuckles white as she squeezed the blunderbuss's barrel.

"We know," Molly had said. "Come quickly!"

When they hung up, Marlow pocketed the phone and returned to the front room where Boris and Bryony were saying their farewells. Marlow watched Dan asleep on the couch. The boy who was inadvertently responsible for the encroaching end of the world and for bringing Marlow closer to her estranged family.

"Bloody kids," Marlow had mumbled, throwing her back-pack over her shoulder.

"I pray you know what you're doing," said Boris as he followed her outside, pausing only to rub Dan affectionately on the head.

"Sure I do…"

"I THOUGHT YOU HAD A PLAN!" Boris yelped as Marlow grabbed the man's lapels and dragged his head below the cover afforded by the van just as a nine-legged insectoid creature scuttled past. It resembled a praying mantis with writhing spiked arms. Blood dripped from its maw, and Marlow regretted staring hard enough to notice the remains of somebody's foot lodged between its mandibles.

As it drew close, it suddenly stopped. Compound eyes scanned the wreckage for more food as its jaws clicked rapidly together. Boris peeked from behind the vehicle and gasped. The faint noise was enough to catch the creature's attention. Its head snapped sharply in their direction and the clicking stopped. It cocked its head quizzically, then bobbed low as it cautiously approached.

Marlow's hand clamped across Boris's mouth as he whimpered in fright. She increased the pressure as the creature drew close. "Shut up," she growled - but it was too late. The beast had heard them. It clicked excitedly as it gained speed. Marlow risked a look just in time to see its bowed head slam into the door of the van they were hiding behind.

The powerful blow shoved the vehicle sideways. Tyres moved with ease over the snow, pushing Marlow and Boris a few feet before the wheels butted up against the kerb. The creature continued pushing – and the van slowly tipped onto two wheels.

Boris was frozen to the spot, gawking as the vehicle threatened to pancake him. Marlow sprung to the side, gripping Boris' elbow to drag him along – just as the van teetered and fell onto its side with a crunch.

Marlow rolled. Her left knee threatened to give way as she stood in one swift motion. The Infiltrator leapt on top of the van. Its siren roar was louder than ever as it shot a pair of scything limbs at lightning speed in a series of experimental punches that could decapitate anything within reach.

But Marlow still had her edge. The blunderbuss's stock rested against her cheek as she nestled it against her shoulder and fired. There was no need to aim - not with the close proximity of her target.

Dozens of pellets split the Infiltrator apart in a shower of blue gore. The hole in its chest was so wide the torso ripped in two.

"I can't believe it was so close," whispered Boris.

Marlow pulled Boris by the arm and they marched across the street. She constantly checked for an attack from any direction. "After a noise like that, we'll be seeing a bunch more real close soon. Move it!"

They crouch-ran across the street, Marlow's boots trampling the creature's evaporating remains. The snowfall increased as they made progress through several adjacent roads, cautiously peering around each corner to check the coast was clear.

Ahead, their destination loomed. The rip between worlds was expanding, and the view beyond it was a hybrid between the engulfed town and the Nightmare realm, dominated by jagged mountains. Unidentifiable growths covered every building on the periphery of the tear and vehicles were cocooned in tough gelatinous shells. The material pulsed under Marlow's fingers as if it were alive, or at least a hitherto unknown version of life. More biomechanical gunk dripped from buildings and crisscrossed the streets like a fungus. As they advanced, the human screams diminished until all they could hear was a cacophony of chittering.

Boris did not say another word, even when they were forced to roll under a lorry as a gigantic *thing* undulated past them, leaving a trail of hissing slime. The creature had been so tall that they couldn't see the top of the slug body that towered above the homes on either side of them. It paused only to eject the putrid smelling biomechanical ooze over several nearby vehicles to cocoon them. Once the immediate danger had passed, they headed to the end of the road, which opened up into the main high street.

Here, everything was covered in the tough organic substance. Snow was already settling on it and it cracked like bubble wrap when stepped on, making a stealthy approach impossible. Festive decorations were coated in gunk, the Christmas tree in the middle of the street had been chewed in half - the displaced section landing through a clothing store window. It was here they also saw the first signs of what had happened to the missing population.

Ant-like creatures, each about the size of a refrigerator, sprouting a mass of seething tentacles across their backs, hauled large biomechanical crystal shards down the main thoroughfare. Marlow had first assumed they were carrying some kind of Infiltrator junk, until Boris pointed out movement from within the semi-transparent shards. They watched in mute horror as a human hand pressed against the opaque cocoon wall, trying to claw their way out.

"There're thousands of them," whispered Boris, his voice cracking. "What are they doing with them all?"

Marlow knew the Infiltrators were ruthless predators, but she never thought they killed for food, just for hatred. Then again, Infiltrator biology was an area nobody had investigated. She was reminded how close the Infiltrators had been to her children - right outside their door. It was heartbreaking to think their lives were at risk, but it was somehow more alarming that they were being kept alive for some unsavoury, or even *savoury*, reason. Somehow that seemed worse than a quick death. She gently patted her jacket, feeling Dan's mobile phone inside. She could still call them...

"Where are they taking them?" Boris repeated. Marlow broke from her muse and shrugged, a gesture that irritated Boris. "Do you know *anything?*" He turned back to the line of creatures carrying their victims to the end of the street, through the portal, and into the twisted reality beyond. "We must free them."

"Are you nuts? There're thousands of them! How long do you think we could stand up to that many Infiltrators while we hack open them pods? Thirty seconds? A minute? And they look just like workers. What if they call for reinforcements, some of the big suckers back there? We'd be dead before we broke the first person out."

Boris sighed, Marlow was right, but that didn't mean he had to like it. "So how do we get the Darkmare to come out?"

Marlow hadn't thought that far ahead, she'd been more focused on avoiding the critters in the street, but now they were here the major problem had revealed itself.

"Well... I was kinda hoping harsh language might've lured it out," said Marlow lamely.

"Tell me you're joking?"

The truth was the plan had sounded feasible back in her father's cottage, but they hadn't factored in the host of Infiltrators occupying the town. The scale of the invasion was shocking.

"Then we have to go to it."

Marlow shook her head. "Can't be done. No human can cross. It's like a waking dream over there. You could Astral Walk, but you'd have to be asleep and then the Darkmare would have control over you."

"So we just sit here and wait?" snapped Boris irritably.

Marlow watched the creatures' movements, identifying routes around them towards the shimmering wall between realities which now a gap half a mile wide, severing the town in half as it accepted a constant train of captives going in.

"Those people're alive in there," she mused.

"Yeah, so?"

"So the cocoon must protect them." She was thinking

about something Dan had said, then thought about her father's lab.

Boris snickered hopelessly. "You want to hide in a pod? Wonderful idea. That's assuming they don't kill you on sight or that you can hack your way out from the inside. I don't see many people escaping, do you?"

"The Infiltrators infect their Conduit's mind with a calming sedative. It acts as a lubrication between worlds and allows the beast to open the portal to come through."

"So?"

"So, if we can get some of that... perhaps we can get through there," she nodded towards the portal.

Boris frowned. "And where exactly do you get this sedative?"

MARLOW'S MIDNIGHT blade cleaved through the Infiltrator's neck. The creature collapsed, crystalizing as it fell into the snow. Marlow dropped the blade and caught the beast's head to prevent it from shattering on the pavement.

They had retraced their steps until they came across a patrolling Infiltrator, one of sufficiently small size that Marlow felt comfortable to ambush. Luckily, it hadn't taken long.

Boris stared at the head. "So, where exactly is this sedative stored?"

Marlow carefully laid the head in the snow and used her blade to chip through the creature's beetle-shaped head. It splintered like candy and Boris took a step back in repulsion as she exposed the gelatinous brain which gave a fishy scent.

With a crunch, Marlow peeled a section of skull away, which crumbled in her fingers. Inside the skull cavity was an oval rubbery sac. Through the thin membrane the same electric blue ooze she had seen in her father's lab was visible. She carefully held it up for Boris to see, keeping one hand over as protection from the falling snow.

"And what exactly do we do with that?" asked Boris. "Daub ourselves in it so we glow in the dark?"

"Don't be dumb. We drink it."

For a moment Boris said nothing. He expected Marlow to add a punch line. When he saw the Hunter was serious, he grimaced. "You're insane."

"The Infiltrators administer this stuff straight in your noggin'," said Marlow tapping Boris' forehead. "The best way of getting it in there I can think of is to drink it. Then we can go right thought to the other side." She hesitated. "In theory."

"What if we don't go?" he mumbled quietly. Marlow studied Boris's pale face. "I mean, what do we really expect to do once we're through there?"

"Find the Darkmare and kill it."

Boris couldn't meet her gaze and focused on his own feet. "We should have tried to wake, Dan. I mean, if he is responsible for opening this... if we just wake him..."

"Dan's body is asleep, but his mind ain't home. Understand?"

Boris's jaw muscles worked overtime. "I keep thinking of Bryony. My daughter's alone with him. If anything..."

"She ain't alone, that copper's with her."

Boris rolled his eyes. "She doesn't know what to do!"

"Listen, Dan's mind is in Innerspace right now." Marlow pointed towards the portal beyond the smothered buildings. "Through there. Remember your dreams as a kid? No matter how nice they seemed, what you recall is a distorted version of that place there. There you can create anything, be anyone..." She stared at the reality rip fully aware of the irony that she had never had a dream in her life, yet was about to walk across the threshold into a waking nightmare. The very first she would experience, and in all probability, the very last.

Boris's voice was nothing more than a whisper. "What if you're wrong?"

"Then we'll fry to dead trying to cross over."

Marlow studied him for several moments. Boris was clearly on the edge of a breakdown fuelled by raw fear. He would be a useless sidekick in his current state, and Marlow couldn't imagine him getting any better. As usual, she was being left down, forced to face the horrors alone. Nothing new, except this time she felt no bitterness. Marlow had no doubts that passing into the abyss was the only way to save her own children, Trebor. She was doing it for them – not for money. She recognised that in Boris, beneath the dread was genuine concern for his family that outweighed personal safety and it was driven by regret.

Empathy, she thought, *that's what it's called.* She had read about it once, but now she understood. After all, she was not only doing this just for her own family, but for Dan too.

"Dammit," she swore aloud. She had no desire to go alone, but a part of her needed to make sure the kid was safe. "You're right. You should be with them. Make sure they're OK." The relief flooding across Boris's face was instant. "Just keep your head low and don't engage any Infiltrator in a fight. You see one, run or hide." Boris nodded. Marlow caught his arm. "And just in case..." she trailed off, unsure how to describe her own imminent death, "Y'know... find my family. Get them out."

Boris solemnly shook her hand. "I promise. Good luck."

Marlow watched Boris disappear back the way they came, never once looking back. She wanted to hate him, but couldn't muster the energy required to be so cynical. Instead she poked a hole through the delicate sac she'd scooped from the Infiltrator's brain and put it to her lips. It smelled like off seafood.

"Cheers," she muttered, then knocked the thick fluid back. It was an unpleasant sensation to feel the ice cold gunk slowly flow across her tongue and slither down her throat. She coughed, almost choking, and grabbed a handful of snow to chase the brain-fluid down.

The taste lingered in her mouth, but it hadn't killed her. She retraced her steps back towards the portal. Getting past the Infiltrator Workers and through the gap would be easy. She just hoped Dan's speculative idea about crossing to the other side would work.

Without another thought, Marlow sprinted forward, intent on saving the world and hoping she wouldn't be sick along the way.

CHAPTER SIXTEEN

BRYONY DABBED A DRIPPING cool flannel against her son's head. In the last few minutes he had whimpered and twitched as he broke into a fever. Behind his closed lids, his eyes wheeled around in REM sleep. She tried to wake him several times by talking and rocking him, but she had refrained from being too rough or making loud noises. She'd read on the internet that waking a sleepwalker could kill them, but wasn't sure how true that was. In the state Dan was in, she had no desire to find out.

Officer Janet had locked every door she could, even using a sideboard to barricade the door that connected the living room to the kitchen. "Too many entry points," she kept mumbling.

The power was still on, the room's main lights and the blinking Christmas tree creating more pools of darkness than they banished. Marlow's warnings about the shadows were fresh in their mind, but with the creatures now freely walking the world, neither woman thought that was an issue anymore. The terrible noises outside had diminished since

Boris and Marlow had left, and they entered a phase of uneasy hope...

Which was shattered when a loud crash outside drew their attention to the window in time to see a flaming car roll down the street, shedding bodywork as it rushed by.

"Wait there," whispered Officer Janet as she edged closer to the window and pressed her face against the glass. She could see enormous dark shadows moving at the end of the street. Even through the double-glazing, she could hear anguished screams chillingly cut to silence.

They were here.

She darted for the lights, plunging the house into darkness. Only the Christmas tree illuminations still danced.

"Turn them off!" she hissed. "If it's dark they might not think we're here." She peeked through the window and saw inhuman figures heading in their direction. "Hurry!"

It took several precious seconds for Bryony's groping hand to pull the plug out, extinguishing the tree lights. Just in time as a spindly irregular shadow crossed the window outside.

They both held their breath as an explorative tapping scrambled against the door. Thank God they had locked everything.

Bryony crooked her head so she could isolate the direction the noise was coming from. It had stopped - replaced with the low squeak of an opening door.

With increasing horror, Bryony recognised the sound of the backdoor...

THE TRANSITION between realities was a lot like falling up, down and sideways at the same time.

Marlow experienced the *falling jolt* dreamers did before they abruptly awoke. It was as if gravity between the two worlds didn't quite line up. To her relief, the brain fluid she had drank worked, and she hadn't been burned alive crossing into the Nightmare Realm. She felt lighter and more agile the moment she passed the cool shimmering screen of air, and equated it as a taste of what life would be like with regular exercise.

"I'm in a dream," she chuckled to herself, not quite believing it and trying to ignore the fact that a 'waking nightmare' was a more accurate description. The air tasted metallic and made her light-headed, almost euphoric. It would be easy to lose one's senses here. She forced herself to focus on the task in hand. She was the first waking person to step foot in the dark world and experienced a glow of pride, having finally earned a place in Cornelius' history.

The realm beyond resembled a poor Dali-like reconstruction of her own world it was consuming. Everything was covered in a disgusting crystalline membrane, which made familiar shapes, such as buildings or vehicles, appear jagged and unsettling. The sky was dark, yet a purple omnipresent light fell across the land.

The convoy of trapped humans continued marching towards a vast structure in the distance, one that towered above the buildings around it and was not part of the original town, constructed from the same biomechanical resin that smothered the landscape and from this distance reminded Marlow of a huge stadium.

With no other hint of where to go, she approached the tower.

CHRISTMAS DECORATIONS MADE POOR WEAPONS, Bryony concluded as she wielded a two-foot ceramic snowman. At least the dangling cable made a handy whip.

Trusting that Dan was too precious for the Infiltrators to harm, she and Officer Janet, armed with a leg broken from the newly repaired coffee table, padded through the open living room doorway into the dark corridor. Normally the streetlight outside provided enough illumination to navigate by, but now only flames danced in the chaos outside. They paused at the foot of the stairs and strained to listen over the throb of their own heartbeats.

Upstairs was silent. A clattering pot from behind the closed kitchen door confirmed there was an intruder. The policewoman took the lead.

Perhaps they can't open doors? Bryony thought in desperation as she stepped closer, snowman raised. *No, they smash through them.*

When Office Janet reached the door, she hesitated and closed her eyes, taking a deep breath to steady her nerves. Her hand fell on the door handle. They could clearly hear the sound of something scuffling across the tiles beyond. Bryony raised the snowman and wished that her father hadn't gone with the ghastly Nightmare Hunter.

Fearing she would lose her nerve at any moment, Officer Janet put all her weight on the door as she twisted the handle, at the same time unleashing a wild scream of angst she wasn't aware she was storing.

Bryony charged forward, screaming: "Get out of my home!"

They saw movement in the darkness. Bryony swung the snowman by the cable flex with all her strength. It whirled past her ear and arced down on the beast with a sharp clash of fracturing ceramic. Now free of the cumbersome snowman, the electrical cable cracked like a whip and she swung it around for another strike. The intruder dropped to the floor with a loud thump.

"Stop!" the policewoman yelled.

Bryony groped for the light switch, the ancient fluorescent tube buzzing loudly as flicked to life after several false starts. They took the crime scene in with a single glance: the open back door - with a key in the lock. What kind of monster uses a key? Her victorious smile froze when she remembered that the nightmares didn't wear clothes; particularly not familiar fleece coats.

Bryony kneeled and rolled the prone body over.

"Dad?" Blood trickled from a scalp wound. What had she done?

The officer cradled Boris's head, feeling for a pulse. "He's concussed," she said before an ear-splitting gurgling roar came from the darkness of the garden beyond. A dozen cobalt eyes appeared and a mass of flickering ebony tentacles filled the doorway.

A limb shot out and stuck to Officer Janet like glue. Then it yanked her outside. She didn't even have time to scream – but the sound of crunching bones was unmistakable.

MARLOW HAD NEVER BEEN to Rome. She had never have the chance to travel abroad, yet another regret in her life that she would never have time to rectify. But she'd seen pictures and what she thought was a stadium. On closer inspection, more closely resembled the Coliseum constructed from the Infiltrators' biomechanical resin.

She had discreetly followed the line of humans here and watched the worker drones enter the structure through an archway. Further archways pocked the nightmarish Coliseum's curving façade, and she could see both sky and movement beyond, confirming her suspicions that it was hollow within.

An unholy cacophony rose from the arena. Marlow was

accustomed to the Infiltrators' high-pitch chittering, but this was a deep and sonorous that chilled to the core. The only way in, avoiding the workers, was through the archways higher up and that meant climbing.

Marlow shouldered the blunderbuss and pulled the strap tight. She reached as high as she could, fingers finding solid purchase on the pitted surface. The resin offered plenty of nooks and she shoved her steel toecaps firmly in and hoisted herself up. Even with her slightly elevated strength, her knees clicked. Not for the first time in the last hour, Marlow wished she were fitter, younger and a million miles from here.

Grunting with every move, Marlow clambered higher. The baseball bat dangling from her waist painfully struck her knee more than once.

What the hell have I become? she thought darkly. She used to be proud and at least moderately attractive - with a wonderful family and the world at her feet. Now she was an unfit alcoholic. She had let everything slip away. She'd always envied those who could dream; who could soar in a realm where anything was possible. Now she was here, she could feel the flip side. The utter despair only a nightmare could induce.

Marlow tried to blank the discouraging thoughts from her mind, now wasn't the time for introspection. She wondered if that what she really felt or was it negative vibes put out by the Darkmare as it fed on human misery.

She suspected the answer lay somewhere between the two.

Don't look down, Marlow told herself as she pressed ever higher. Her rebellious streak took that exact opportunity to look down. She had climbed higher that she'd thought, at least six stories up. Even though she had a firm grip, her palms became clammy and her left knee quaked, threatening to give out. The ground was covered in jagged stalagmites of gunk that threatened certain death if she fell.

Marlow focused on her destination. The archway was only a couple of feet away.

Then her foot slipped. She hadn't moved it and was certain she'd found a secure niche, but the ledge suddenly crumbled away - exactly as it should in all good nightmares.

Marlow fell.

The sensation was brief. One second she was dropping - the very next she was hanging from a noose and choking as the blunderbuss's strap caught on a snarl of resin. The antique weapon was now bearing all her weight. She scrambled across the pitted surface and drew closer to the coliseum's facade, taking the pressure from her neck. A simple shoulder shrug dislodged the strap, and she could breathe once again.

Her fingers probed the archway above and found a rim as wide as a windowsill. With aching arms, Marlow hauled herself onto a narrow ledge eighteen inches across, providing a safe perch to catch her breath. It offered a spectacular view into the unearthly arena beyond.

The circular open-air amphitheatre soared forty storeys to jagged spires that twisted to the sky like demonic conical shells. Alcoves pitted the walls at random intervals around the structure, constructed with a chaotic design ethic in mind.

Towards the base of the walls, the structure tiered inwards in an unusual bleacher formation, which was filled with human containment shards. A third of the arena was already covered in cocoons that, from Marlow's vantage point, resembled tiny brown pills. She estimated there were at least twenty thousand – which meant at least a quarter of the town was already here, stacked in small pyramids by the worker drones. This was all assessed in seconds as her gaze swept the arena towards the thing at the far end. Towering some ten storeys was the Dark-mare. It was unmistakable.

An ovoid creature dripped ooze and bile from pores the

size of her head, however the stench was pleasant, like a field
of violets. Tentacles flapped from the main body and stretched
like bungee cords. An enormous mouth cleaved the stomach
vertically, a million barbed teeth grinding together. A crown of
spider-like eyes, as black as midnight, circled the mushroom-
shaped head, allowing it to see in all directions at once.

As Marlow studied the horror, she noticed puss-filled
bulges around the Darkmare's base swelled and popped like
wet blisters, Infiltrators fell out in a splash of fluid. Creatures
of all shapes and sizes. Their limbs flailed like newborn calves
as they struggled to find their feet, if they had any. It didn't
take long for them to shake the amniotic fluid off their cara-
paces and become fully formed killers that scuttled from the
arena. There were thousands of them.

Marlow's heart sank. She tried to recall any useful nugget
of information her father had shared... but all she could recall
were the repetitive exercises of where to strike the Infiltrators
to puncture their toughened skulls. Not terribly useful information when faced with an ever-increasing army of
monstrosities.

Then she noticed movement on an elevated dais, just
behind the Darkmare. At first Marlow assumed it was another
beast, but the shape stood out from the twisted surroundings.
It was a boy. Marlow rubbed her eyes. She couldn't believe
what she was seeing, but there was no mistaking it.

It was Dan.

BRYONY'S first instinct was to kick the door against the beast
but it rebounded from the flopping rubbery limbs lunging
inside, and a gnarled tusk protruding from the creature's jaw
smashed through the double-glazed window.

Her feet slipped on the linoleum floor, made slicker by the

snow melting off Boris's coat and the phlegm that spat from the Infiltrator as it roared. Bryony was on her hands and knees as she pulled Boris towards the hallway. She was not a physically strong, but the need to protect her family provided all the strength she needed to make it to the next door.

Slapping heavy tentacles chased them across the floor, each ending in tiny beaks that hungrily snapped for flesh. Luckily, the back door was too small for the monster to press its bulk through.

Once she had dragged Boris into the hallway, she booted the door shut - so hard it severed a smaller tentacle. The limb exploded into slush as it hit the floor, staining the carpet a deep maroon. Standing, she could more easily drag her father into the living room and dropped him next to Dan, still happily slumbering on the couch.

The kitchen door would provide little protection from the intruder, neither would the living room door, but she slammed it closed too. She rolled the reclining armchair against the living room door for good measure.

She covered her ears to block out the crashing sounds from the kitchen and what sounded like the kitchen door splintering apart. She had to get out, but how? Boris was unconscious and Dan was still in a coma.

The unmistakable sound of collapsing bricks came from the kitchen. The beast was demolishing the house. Then the dark room suddenly got darker. It took a second for Bryony to realise that the ambient light from outside was being blocked.

Something was lurking beyond the window.

She held her breath, worried that the faintest sound would attract more trouble. She held on to Marlow's comment that the Infiltrators wouldn't harm Dan. Their Conduit was too precious. But they would have no qualms killing those around him.

The shape outside the window didn't move, and curiosity got the better of her.

Combating fear, she took a step towards the window. A shaking hand reached out for the curtain...

Then, through the crack between the drapes, a blazing circular blue eye the size of a basketball appeared, and peered straight at her.

Bryony was too terrified to scream, but she swore she heard her hair turning white with shock. The beast at the window gave a throaty click that rose in excitement like a runaway Geiger counter. Bryony instinctively stepped back, anticipating the window would shatter at any moment.

They were trapped. Their fate was sealed.

CHAPTER SEVENTEEN

A DREAM... Marlow repeated over and over. Technically, she was in a dream, well, a nightmare, but that meant unexpected things happened. Seeing Dan standing behind the nightmare, laughing and talking to somebody she couldn't quite make out, fitted within that category.

With a groan like an enormous empty stomach wambling, the Darkmare shifted position and a mass of limbs blocked her view of the kid. She crouched in the shadows and tried to plan her next move. Even as she watched, the Darkmare had birthed a dozen Infiltrators. Stalling just increased the odds against her.

A dream... of course!

The Dan she was looking at was his dream-form; what the mind formed when it went Astral Walking in Innerspace. Marlow hated the hokey term, but couldn't think of one better - it was Dan's astral projection acting out the dream he was having. Perhaps Marlow wasn't so alone over here? Judging by the way the Darkmare kept him close, he was pretty important here too.

Marlow scrambled down the archway's tiers into the arena. The uneven surface provided plenty of hand and toeholds, and the shadows provided cover, so it wasn't until she had reached the sloping tiers, with their aisles of prisoner cocoons, did Marlow remember the Infiltrators could just as easily see in the dark.

Dammit, concentrate! She thumped her palm against her forehead to reinforce the point. She had made a career out of being sloppy and now was not the time to continue.

She readied the blunderbuss, unlocking the ancient safety catch which she was never sure worked anyway, just in case she ran nose-to-*labrum* into one critter.

The cocoons towered above her, some twenty layers high - much taller than they had seemed from her earlier vantage point. Opaque forms could be seen inside, thrashing in their own private hells. Suppressing a chill, Marlow ran to the end of one aisle and crouched behind the pyramids. Now she could see the Darkmare was positioned on a raised dais in the centre.

The increasing pile of cocoons stretched a hundred more yards, and the Infiltrator drones were busy at the far end of, stacking yet more bodies. Even without their presence, it wasn't a clear run. The floor leading to the dais spouted corkscrewing stalagmites that glinted in the source-less light. Closer scrutiny revealed they were slowly growing. Wet resin seeped out of the top like candle wax and oozed down the spiralling slopes. It pooled across the floor. A puddle was inching towards Marlow from the nearest spire and it smelled vaguely like... like baking bread.

She checked nothing was watching, then reached across and tapped her index finger in the leading edge of the puddle. It stuck. She pulled hard, but still her finger remained steadfastly secure.

"Dammit!" muttered Marlow. She should have known better. The Infiltrators used sweet smells to beguile their victims. The liquid surrounding the Darkmare was like flypaper sticky enough to trap anybody foolish enough to venture near. She leaned back and pulled, throwing her weight into it. There was a terrible crack as the bones in her index finger dislocated - and a jolt of pain shot through her hand. It was all she could do not to cry out in excruciating agony.

Then she heard the unmistakable clicking of insectoid legs approaching from the adjacent aisle.

Marlow leaned forward just enough to grip her injured finger with her free hand to prevent the bones from dislocating any further. She pulled hard. Tears welled in her eyes as skin tore. She fell back, and couldn't stop the yelp of pain as she held her throbbing red index. The epidermis had been torn away, leaving just an almost transparent coating of skin. She could see the blood beneath. The pain was akin to torture and almost made her pass out.

An Infiltrator suddenly stepped from around the stack. It had its back to Marlow as it inspected the viscous liquid. Marlow slowly crawled backward, the pain in her finger suddenly forgotten. She kept her eyes on the creature, her other hand reaching for the blunderbuss... *where was it?* She must have dropped it when she toppled backward.

Marlow pushed firmly against a cocoon in a desperate attempt to blend in. She was thankful that the monster didn't have a good sense of hearing.

She became acutely aware that there was a shuddering human arm inches from her face, visible through the transparent cocoon. Fresh meat imprisoned in transparent coffins and stacked like cans in a—

The Infiltrator bellowed. With the distraction, Marlow hadn't seen it turn towards her, head cocking like a curious dog to see if she was a threat or not. This critter most resembled an eight-foot tall praying mantis with a long centipede body and dozens of legs snaking behind it. A pair of fat forearms looked like inflated boxing gloves, and a triplet of dangling trunks from its head wriggled as they probed ahead.

Marlow yanked the baseball bat from her waist and swung it threateningly as the monster-spurred forwards. The beast raised an arm to deflect the blow, and the wood shattered in half. Marlow gasped in surprised. She'd had the bat since childhood; a staunch defence from everything that had loomed in the darkness. The attack had made the Infiltrator pause for several seconds, allowing her to scuttle backwards. Her hand touched something metallic and cool: the blunderbuss.

The mantis was still several feet away as she swung the gun around and squeezed the trigger. The moment her sore fingertip touched the stiff trigger, a sharp pain shot through her hand and she dropped the weapon.

She groped to retrieve it as the mantis thumped its forearms together. What Marlow had whimsically thought of as boxing gloves sounded like a wet bell tolling and a wave of air shimmered white as it rolled towards her. The sound wave struck like a wrecking ball, lifting Marlow clean off her feet and throwing her a dozen yards. The high-pitch squeal of tinnitus was deafening.

She had no time for pain. The shock wave had slid her gun closer. She reached for it and missed - her sense of balance was all messed up.

The mantis surged forwards, readying its arms for another volley of audio death.

Marlow lunged for the blunderbuss, remembering to fire it with her other hand as she squeezed the trigger. The boom was deafening, but her aim was true.

A cloud of pellets erupted from the blunderbuss's conical

barrel - shredding the fiend's abdomen in a gory splatter of blue Infiltrator blood. The creature's torso was severed clean off the body. As it fell, the lower body scuttled in a circle before flipping onto its back, legs still kicking.

"Don't mess with the meat," snarled Marlow.

As if in response, the mantis gave a final clap of its arms. Another shock wave burst forth, but this one was weaker than the first and missed Marlow. Instead, it impacted into the pod just behind her, shattering the resin. The cocoons balanced on top were blown from the stack, and the entire structure shook.

"Aw, crap..."

The shuddering pile collapsed like an avalanche, and several hundred cocoons suddenly surged towards her. Marlow dodged past the Infiltrator's severed torso and leapt over the jerking legs in her haste to escape. She ran for her life, gun in one hand. She just had time to figure out the next two looming problems - one: the sticky sap pools lay ahead, and two: she was too unfit to outrun the pursuing landslide of cocooned humans.

BRYONY PITCHED to the floor and crawled on her elbows to reach Dan's side. The sounds of destruction from the kitchen escalated as the rest of the external wall collapsed across the sink. Outside the window there was increasing hints of excited movements, but nothing more defined than black against black. It was just a matter of time before the beasts broke in.

She cradled Dan's head in her lap and considered her choices. Marlow had been adamant that the monsters wouldn't harm Dan, they needed to protect him, which made her and Boris a threat.

She kicked her father with her foot. "Wake up," she hissed

as loud as she dared. He didn't respond; the ceramic snowman must have packed a hell of a punch. She had often wondered how her son developed such a terrible ability. Discovering it was genetic made her furious. Yet, she could only blame herself for ignoring the problem for so long. She had hoped Dan would outgrow the phase just like many kids stopped wetting the bed. But her son's issues had extended from bed wetting, to tearing furniture apart, and through to mass invasion and the possible extinction of mankind. That put things in perspective.

Dan grunted, agitation twisted his face, and he twitched in his sleep. She wondered what he was dreaming about. His forehead was coated in a glaze of sweat; she should wake him. Maybe waking him would dispel the monsters closing in on them... but at what risk? Would the shock of suddenly waking kill him? Or was that an old wives' tale?

Another section of wall collapsed in the kitchen, followed by a gelatinous sound. Bryony imagined that the beast was oozing into the house. Her suspicions were confirmed with scratching on the living room door. Time was running out.

"Dan, wake up!" she gave him a sharp nudge. "Snap out of it! You need to wake up right now, mister, or we're all going to die! Dan? Can you hear me?" Fear was overtaking caution, and she shook him with increasing vigour. Dan spluttered, his lips twisting as if in response... but he replied only with a trail of drool from the corner of his mouth as he rolled onto his side with a whimper.

The living room door shook as it was prodded from behind. Bryony looked around helplessly. She was trapped, defenceless and alone.

She was going to die.

· · ·

THE SURGE of capsules striking Marlow was made worse by the rib she had busted. The resin cases had a plastic feel to them that absorbed some of the impact, but there was nothing she could do to avoid them as they bounced around her in every direction.

She was struck from all angles. A blow to the back of her legs flipped sent her head-over-heels, and she landed across several pods. They rolled underneath her, effectively surfing her over the sticky pools that didn't seem to adhere to the cocoons. The chaos drew the attention of a hundred-or-so Infiltrators milling around the coliseum.

With constant impacts from every direction, Marlow ricocheted between the pods and was deposited on the dais at the foot of the Darkmare. Everything ached as she lay on her back, gazing up at the towering goliath. The beast stopped spawning its vile brethren and its head angled to stare at her. Tentacles thrashed in outrage that an intruder had got so far and it emitted a chilling squeal - literally. Marlow had often flippantly told people how the Infiltrators made the blood run cold, but in this case frost formed over her exposed skin and the gelid atmosphere stung her hand and face, as her body temperature plummeted. Marlow swayed to her feet and looked frantically around for her gun. Then she reached for her katana – but her hand met only empty space. It must have slid from its sheath during the multiple impacts.

The spawning pores across the Darkmare irritably bubbled and frothed, but no newly formed Infiltrator spewed out. The Darkmare seemed to hesitate as its army of Infiltrators, a vast array of shapes, sizes and appendages, stopped their tasks and silently observed. It was a tense stand-off, but Marlow couldn't figure out what the Darkmare was waiting for.

She spotted her blunderbuss on the edge of the platform; precariously hanging over the sea of gloop and fallen cocoons -

at the same time she caught a muffled conversation from behind the Darkmare. Dan emerged, talking to the figure Marlow had seen from afar, who was till obscured behind the nightmare.

"Marlow?" said Dan uncertainly.

Marlow was cautious. She recalled fragments of her father's ramblings about Astral Walkers and wished she'd paid more attention now that her life depended on it. Walkers were the person's subconscious although, through Dan's eyes, he was in a wonderful dream filled with colour and life, rather than the bleak horrors that surrounded him. Dan wouldn't be seeing things correctly. In addition, his own memories would validate the surreal world around him, allowing the dreamer to accept the new reality. Or so Marlow had read. Because she could not dream, it was very difficult to know what Dan was experiencing, so wasn't sure how to handle the situation. It could be like talking to a stranger. She decided to be herself - no, wait - that would be disastrous. She would try to be the *version* of herself she longed to be.

She forced a smile. "Hey, Dan. Good to see you... here." Dan's brow furrowed, his eyes scanning Marlow with suspicion. "You remember your old pal, right?" Marlow prompted.

The look of mistrust on Dan's face deepened. "How can you be here?"

Aware of the hordes of killers around him, and the Master of Nightmares looming above, Marlow strained every muscle until it hurt to smile. "Oh, I was just wandering past and saw ya. Thought it was time to take you home to your mother."

Dan took a step back. Something was clearly amiss. He looked to the figure behind the Darkmare. "I don't want to go with her. I want to stay here with you."

Marlow suddenly remembered another essential fragment of information. Walkers were in their own dream world and could create guardians, familiar faces that populated their dreams. Marlow suspected the figure walking from the shadows was Dan's dream-version of Boris.

"Don't worry, Dan," said the unseen figure. "You ain't going anywhere." It wasn't Boris's voice, it was one laced with menace.

Marlow scrambled for a list of possible people Dan would have conjured up as a mentor – and drew the inevitable conclusion. Marlow's heart sank at the thought of being forced to battle a fake-version of Dan's own father, right in front of the kid.

"Get behind me, Dan," the figure prompted as it moved from the shadows. Dan did so, his gaze never leaving Marlow.

Marlow was poleaxed when she saw the figure. The voice was unfamiliar, but the face wasn't.

She was looking at *herself*.

Or rather, a new and improved version of her. Her hair was washed, straight and it flowed in an invisible breeze. Her skin was perfection, her face serene. Even her perfectly fitting clothes were not covered in a menu of food stains. She was both horrified and flattered that Dan had chosen her as his ultimate protector.

The dream-Marlow eyed her foe critically. "Don't look right, does it? Got the nose wrong for a start, and I ain't so fat and disgusting." Dan giggled as the imposter circled Marlow. "It must be some kind've shape-shifting dream monster."

Marlow surmised that in the Darkmare's influence, Dan couldn't see the beast, or even the other Infiltrators. As far as the kid was concerned, he could be standing at home when the second Marlow appeared.

"Dan, this is not me," said Marlow pointing to her perfect counterpart. "This is a fake, something the Darkmare created to keep you asleep. Can you see the Darkmare?"

Dan looked vaguely in the Darkmare's direction but looked right through it.

"She's talking balls," said the impostor, causing Dan to giggle again. "I'll crack her head open."

Marlow's fists clenched. "Don't you think—"

Her doppelganger punched her across the jaw so hard that Marlow was lifted off her feet and crashed to the floor.

She tasted blood in her mouth as the clone gripped her around the neck and pulled her back to her feet. Marlow hadn't been expecting the speed or strength of the attack. She could barely breathe as the fake angled her left then right, inspecting her closely. Out of sight from Dan, the doppelganger's face bubbled and twisted as it made subtle refinements in its guise.

Marlow felt a punch to her solar plexus with such force, tears streamed from her eyes. She glimpsed Dan's concern before the imposter stood between them.

"Dan..." she gasped, reaching for him. "You're dreaming..."

A heavy boot slammed into Marlow's side and sent her sliding along the dais, through the slick embryonic gloop surrounding the Darkmare.

Marlow knew time was against her. She couldn't survive much more pummelling. She defiantly clambered to her feet, one hand using the cold body of the Darkmare for support as the fake-Marlow bore towards her like a locomotive.

"Dan - *I'm* Marlow, kid. It's me. Think hard... would I really go nuts 'n' beat up someone like this?"

The fake leapt for Marlow - but this time she sidestepped - her foot slipping in gloop, that sent her sprawling once again. She saw Dan looking thoughtful as the imposter took a super-human leap - covering the eighteen-foot gap between them in a single bound.

Once again, the breath was crushed from Marlow, and

more ribs popped as the fraud landed on top of her. She tried to lash out, but the imposter's weight was crushing – and increasing with the inevitability of a nightmare. Her attacker's fists moved so fast they were a blur - and pain exploded across Marlow's back as her kidneys took the brunt.

The fake leaned so close that Marlow could smell its stale fishy breath. "I'll butcher ya right here, Nightmare Killer," it hissed.

Marlow's struggles were futile; the doppelganger was immovable. With a sharp click the 'ganger's right forearm split into two forming scissor-like serrated claws which pressed either side of Marlow's neck.

This is how I buy it, Marlow thought with uncharacteristic calm. *A wasted life and I'm about to be decapitated in someone else's half-dream.*

There was a sickening crunch and a bitter smell. Marlow had once read that the head could stay alive without the body for up to a minute. She fully expected to see her own corpse going into spasm. Instead, the weight shifted off her. It took seconds for Marlow to realise that she was still alive.

She sprang to her feet and rounded on her foe - only to see her split in half all the way down to her stomach. It was a gruesome sight watching herself severed in half, even with the Infiltrators blue crystalline guts spewing out. As the corpse split aside, she saw Dan hefting her katana.

"Faker," he growled and spun the sword with the expert skill only a dreamer possessed. The sword must have fallen when Marlow first fell.

With Marlow's face grotesquely dangling from its split torso, the fraud raced towards Dan. Marlow booted the creature's side – enough to send it straight past Dan and off the dais. The drop was only a couple of feet, but it still shattered with a satisfying crunch.

Marlow peered over the edge to confirm her kill.

"Good riddance."

Then she felt cold steel against her throat. Dan's grip on the sword was unwavering as he slowly stepped into Marlow's field of vision and studied her with deep mistrust.

"How do I know you're real?"

"Welcome back, kid. Good sword, ain't it? Did I ever tell you it was forged from a meteor?"

Dan pressed the blade, and Marlow sucked in a breath.

"Easy, kid. Unlike our pal there, I ain't no figment of your imagination." Uncertainty wavered across Dan's face as he glanced down at the rapidly dissolving remains. "The Darkmare made you create it in the form of somebody you trust. Somebody you c-care about," the words almost choked her. "You can see the Darkmare, right?" She didn't move, only look upwards.

Dan quickly followed her gaze but shook his head.

"You're in a dream... kinda. You're seeing what you want to see. The Darkmare is convincing you you're someplace safe coz it needs you asleep." Dan took a deep breath, trying to work things out. "Remember our plan?" Marlow still didn't dare move, but saw the army of Infiltrators were still keeping back, watching expectantly. She could even see the Darkmare had stopped moving, waiting for the outcome.

"How can this be a dream?" whispered Dan almost to himself.

"By keeping you asleep, it's able to open a rift into our world. You're really back home, with your mum."

"My mum...?" whispered Dan again. "I'd almost forgotten about her." He moved the sword away, letting it hang from his side.

Marlow moved slowly backwards and gently rubbed her neck. "In your dream you can create whatever you want. You once told me how cool it was to suddenly realise you were dreaming so you could create anything you wanted. Me... I never dreamed before."

"Lucid dreaming. I remember."

"Good, good. Keep on remembering."

Dan looked around. His frown was still in place, but she could see the veil of fog lifting from his perception.

"The Darkmare," he whispered as he kept slowly turning around. "It wouldn't be that massive thing towering over us, would it?"

Marlow could barely stop the grin spreading across her face. "Oh, so you can see it. Good start. That means you can wake up."

The ground suddenly shook with such violence that cracks spread across the dais. What Marlow had first thought was an earthquake was the Darkmare booming roaring as it felt Dan slip from its clutches. Every limb thrashed in frustration.

"It knows you can wake up!" shouted Marlow. "So hurry up and do it! Unlike you, I ain't dreaming. This is very real!"

"How?" shouted Dan over the rumbling bellow.

Before Marlow could answer, the Darkmare swung a tentacle the size of a Redwood at him. Marlow braced herself and instinctively held up her arm, palms outstretched in an odd gesture.

"What're you doing?" screamed Dan as he backed away.

"Trying to create a shield!" shouted Marlow. "You said you can create stuff in your dreams!"

"But you said you're not dreaming!"

The Darkmare's tremendous limb was feet away – hurtling down with lethal force. The last thing she heard was Dan screaming:

"Nnnnoooo!!"

CHAPTER EIGHTEEN

BRYONY SCREAMED LOUDLY. It was the last line of defence she had as the living room door broke into matchsticks and the window imploded as the two Infiltrators closed in on her.

At that exact moment, Dan's entire body flexed, and he sprung from the sofa as if he'd been electrocuted. His unexpected movement escalated Bryony's screams as, with the reflexes of a cat, Dan landed on his feet just as a leathery arm shot into through the window. Its target had been Bryony, but now Dan stood in the way and the Infiltrator's arm suddenly jinked to the side. It scraped a gouge across the wall in a desperate attempt not to hurt him.

A tentacle from the doorway was around Bryony's ankle when Dan spun around and snagged a jagged spare of wood that had been the coffee table and brought it down with all the force he could muster.

The Infiltrator screeched as the stake impaled the sensitive limb. There was no way the tiny weapon could inflict any real damage, yet the tentacle rapidly recoiled and both Infiltrators swiftly disappeared.

"Dan!" His mother hugged him tight. He allowed himself a moment to enjoy the embrace. "Thank goodness you're OK."

Dan pulled away. Something in his memory was vying for attention, but traces of his dream were already vanishing like fog. He noticed his Grandpa on the floor and crossed to him, gently stroking his forehead. "What happened?"

Bryony hesitated. "One of those monsters hit him over the head."

"Grandpa, wake up!" said Dan, shaking him.

"He's unconscious, not asleep." A roar erupted outside, followed by tumbling masonry. Bryony peered through the broken window as snow flurries blew inside. She saw the corner house collapse to rubble as the leathery-armed Infiltrator fled into another street. "Why are they still here? I thought they were supposed to vanish when you woke up?"

Dan joined her, his mind racing. Purple clouds expanded over the town centre; the portal between worlds was still open. That meant Marlow was inside, but was she still alive?

Already details from the dream world were dissolving from his memory. The harder he tried to hold on to them, the quicker they slipped from his mental grasp. It was a dream... he was at home... a home like this but bigger, nicer... and his father... no, not his father.

Marlow! Yes, that was it, Marlow was there but with dream-logic she was also his dad and they were playing football in the sun and...

He couldn't remember. "Think!" he yelled out loud. It did the trick. A fragment of his dream jogged back into place.

A second Marlow had appeared. There had been a fight... the *real* Marlow had come to save him. But then the Darkmare attacked. The details were sketchy again. Dan had run to help Marlow, moving at such an impossible speed he had positioned himself between them...

But what had happened? Dan couldn't recall any detail other than the sensation of falling. Shards of memory slotted together. He had fallen from the platform. His stomach had lurched and seconds before impact...

He had woken up.

So the nightmare should have ended, yet it was still happening around them. Infiltrators were still seeping into the world. Somehow the Darkmare had kept the portal open. But how?

"Marlow's in trouble. We need to help her."

"She can look after herself. We are leaving town," Bryony began searching Boris's trousers for the car keys. "We can drive out of here!" Their car was one of the few outside that wasn't trampled. "You'll have to help me carry Grandpa."

The solution snuck up on Dan. One second he was wondering how the Darkmare was succeeding - and the next he knew. He also knew how to defeat it.

"It's Grandpa."

"That's right," Bryony lifted Boris's arms. "Get his feet."

Dan didn't move; the plan was still crystallising in his mind's eye. "I inherited this from Grandpa. He's now the one keeping the portal open! Because he's unconscious, it's staying open. Don't you see?" Bryony shook her head, lost. "He doesn't have to Astral Walk. He's unconscious, already trapped between worlds. The Darkmare can keep him like this... he'll *never* wake up. The portal wasn't just because of me - either of us could open it, like a shared dream. I still feel part of it, even if I'm awake. It's weird..."

Bryony dropped Boris's arms, and he crumpled back into a heap on the ground, his head cracking on the floor. "Sorry!" she gasped, kneeling to rub her father's head. "I have no idea what you're rambling on about!"

"I've got to find Marlow, then we can stop all this."

"No, Dan! You're back here and you're coming with me."

"Sorry, mum. I can't." He gestured to Boris. "Take him away from here. Go as fast and as far as you can. I'm still half asleep - and I've got to save the world."

Dan didn't even hesitate as he vaulted through the smashed living room window and out into the darkness.

BEING dead wasn't so bad, Marlow had to admit. Sure, every bone, muscle and nerve ending in her body throbbed painfully, but it could have been worse. She wasn't sure what constituted *'worse'*, but she was pretty sure the lack of breathing was on that list.

Breathing... if she was breathing then she couldn't be dead. Marlow pulled herself together; now wasn't the time for a philosophical discussion with herself. She'd only end up losing.

The Darkmare's flailing limb had rushed towards her. She'd raised her arms and willed a shield to appear - only to realize that creation was the privilege of those who dreamed. Just when she was about to die, Dan has reacted with superhuman speed. There was a shimmer of light and Dan had created a shield of pure silver, which the Darkmare had struck.

While it absorbed much of the impact, the punch had still swept Dan and Marlow off the edge of the dais. As she had been tossed in the air like a rag doll, another snake-like appendage had plucked her from the zenith of his arc and drew her to the Darkmare's colossal mouth. Jagged teeth the size of car doors had gashed inches from her face as she was tossed into the mouth.

The teeth slammed down behind her, tearing her trailing jacket, and she was suddenly falling. That's when she lost consciousness.

So, she was now inside the Darkmare's gullet. That would explain the darkness, the smell and the rancid liquid she felt sloshing around her. Marlow reached out and felt several spherical shapes with holes in. They were solid, but covered in a wet material. She suddenly recoiled – they were skulls. Human ones.

Her hand sloshed through other debris - most of which she desperately tried not to identify - before her fingers fell on cold steel. It was a gun. She traced the long barrel as it widened to the end... it was her blunderbuss. The Darkmare must have eaten everything on the dais.

Now we're getting' somewhere, she thought with mounting relief. *Now to find a way out.*

THE COLD AIR stung his lungs as Dan ran through the streets. There was an eerie calm over the town. The ruined streets were devoid of any life: not a single person, pet or Infiltrator.

It was snowing heavier than ever, and Dan regretted running from his home without putting on anything warmer than his t-shirt. He paused to catch his breath and enjoy the heat from a burning van. He oriented himself, which was difficult with no streetlights. Only the purple glow from the portal provided a form of illumination.

After rubbing the warmth back into his hands, he prepared to run again - but suddenly stopped. There was something crunching in the snow. Something was approaching. He hunkered down as close as he dared around the burning vehicle.

The first thing he saw was a shadow, instantly betraying the Infiltrator's fearsome shape. He had assumed they'd all returned to the Coliseum, commanded by some intangible signal from the Darkmare. Perhaps this was a sentry. The Infiltrator appeared at the road junction. It was twice Dan's height and bore a resemblance to a heavily armoured cockroach, walking on five legs. A pair of forearms were raised like gun barrels that dripped green ooze. Antenna on its head twitched as it sampled the air.

Dan didn't move as the creature's head slowly swept the junction - fixing on the burning wreckage. An excited click reverberated in its throat. It had sensed Dan.

There was no point in hiding, so Dan stepped from around the vehicle displaying more courage than he felt. He was unarmed, alone and hopelessly outmatched.

"You know who I am?" The Infiltrator hesitated, its head cocking rapidly left and right as it tried to work out what to do. "That's right. You can't touch me, can you? I'm too valuable." That was his ace card.

The creature stepped forward, drooling mandibles clacking together. Dan bravely held his ground. The creature raised its forearms at him. With a retching sound, liquid spheres shot at him. Dan rolled aside, the snow softening his fall as the liquid splashed across the van and immediately started dissolving the burning metal.

"No! I'm valuable!" warbled Dan as he clambered on his feet.

The acid shooters tracked onto him and fired - once again narrowly missing. Droplets splashed onto his t-shirt and burnt through to his skin. The pain was searing. He hefted snow over the burn to cool it. It was the time to put his theory to the test. It was a long shot, and he felt stupid for not trying it when his life didn't depend on it.

With a terrible wet belch, the monster fired again. Dan raised his arm - and to his own amazement a shield materialised just in time to stop the acid barrage. It was solid and heavy and felt every inch real. The liquid hissed and bubbled on the shield, but failed to make a dent. At the same time, Dan's other hand arced around. The air shimmered around his fist and he was suddenly holding a duplicate of Marlow's katana as if it had always been there.

The Infiltrator yelped in confusion as the blade lobbed off both its forearms, the wound crystallising in an instant. It bellowed in rage, but Dan quickly silenced it with a backswing - decapitating the beast. The head shattered into fragments as it bounded into the van.

Dan whooped victoriously as he expertly whirled the sword in his hand. Then, in the blink of an eye, both sword and shield ceased to be. He was relieved that his theory held true; he was half in the dream he'd opened with his Grandpa. Although awake, he had scored certain privileges while the portal was open. It was a two-way street. The Infiltrators could walk out of the netherworld; and he could operate as if he was some sort of dream warrior inside it.

Dream Warrior - he liked the sound of that.

THE SOUND of the blunderbuss deafened Marlow. After the initial shot, all she could hear was a high-pitched tinnitus that hadn't cleared from earlier. The flash from the barrel briefly lit up a chamber of horrors: bodies of townsfolk and pets in various states of digestion were heaped around. The floor was a seething, bubbling mass of stomach acids, which must have been very mild as Marlow was still in one piece - and the walls were a slimy mass of black flesh that heaved as the Darkmare breathed, except where Marlow's point-blank shot had torn a gaping hole through to the world beyond.

Like pulling the plug out of the bath, Marlow and the unfortunate victims were swept out of the stomach and spilled onto the dais in a tidal wave of vomit. The katana skated past her. She gripped the blunderbuss tightly, sliding on her back away from the Darkmare. The giant thrashed in agony. It was no doubt roaring too - but all she could hear was a monotonous whine that hurt her ears.

It was as if time slowed. Marlow saw the wall of Infiltrators around her surge forward to protect their master. Against countless opponents, she didn't stand a chance.

One Cornelius against the world. It was her family's duty to slay the beast.

Still sliding, Marlow reloaded the gun. She used her heel to brake as she neared the dais edge, but it slowed her only a little. Her heart was in her throat - this close, and from this angle, she had the perfect shot.

Her miserable childhood rushed past her eyes - each little vignette of Carlos forcing her to read the handwritten Hunting tomes, the macabre denizens described within, until she could recite every line. Each minutely detailed picture had been indelibly burned into her mind's eye. Never before had she truly appreciated the attention to detail her forefathers had captured with mere ink. And now here was the Darkmare - every detail captured from vague sightings her father had made. Only now, at the foot of the beast, could she truly appreciate his attention to detail.

Far above, the ring of eyes on the mushroom head, as dead as a shark's. The huge vertical slit of a mouth that had devoured her once already, opened again. Just above the eyes, recessed in the Darkmare's overhanging crown, was a blue band that throbbed like jelly. It was the brain cavity - or so Carlos had indicated on the page. An Infiltrator's fundamental weakness, and she suspected it was the Darkmare's only one.

Marlow couldn't aim as she was still sliding too quickly, but the blunderbuss was not a precision tool and she'd always been good at trigonometry and angles. All she had to do was point and click.

She heard the report from the barrel through her arm. She felt the recoil as she propelled off the dais and into the surrounding resin pond.

Her shot couldn't have been more perfect.

The top of the Darkmare's head split open like a cantaloupe. Foul blue ichor dribbled from within. The creature violently trembled.

Marlow skidded through the sticky volcanoes, but instead of trapping her, the coating of Darkmare's stomach gunk acted as lubrication and she sailed effortlessly through.

The Darkmare toppled backwards into the wall of the coliseum.

The brute's weight shattered the resin walls and cracks raced out in all directions. As the beast quivered in its last death throes, the entire arena began shattering. Massive chunks toppled onto the Infiltrators below, crushing and impaling those too slow to scatter. The ground beneath the remaining cocoon-pyramids fractured, and the piles collapsed, bowling into yet more Infiltrators.

Marlow skidded to a halt against a mean-looking insectoid nightmare. Its flat head rotated towards Marlow and it jabbed a barbed arm at her. Unable to reload, Marlow parried the arm with the blunderbuss - which was violently knocked from her hand. Fight-or-flight kicked in as her flailing hand improbably landed on the hilt of her katana — *with all the luck of a dream,* she thought.

She roiled to her feet as a dozen Infiltrators surrounded her. Closing ranks with an assortment of lethal appendages and slobbering mandibles.

Marlow swung the sword, decapitating one ‒ and then another. A volley of fists, tentacles, feet, forearms and several unidentifiable body parts struck her in rapid succession. She was too weak to put up a real fight. Her sword dropped as she felt her arm break from a savage blow. The pain was so intense she briefly blacked out, only to wake on the floor as she was punched again. She could taste her own blood, but the pain faded from each impact; even her tinnitus faded. It felt as if she was being removed from reality. That's what death must feel like.

An ugly five-legged Infiltrator straddled over her and readied a killing blow through her chest. Then something distracted it‒

Other Infiltrators were tossed in the air with such force they shattered as they struck the floor.

Carving a path through them was Dan, his shield in one hand and a sword in the other. He was whirling and pivoting with impossible speed and grace. Infiltrators were smashed aside with his shield, others stabbed with such acute precision they shattered where they stood. The kid resembled some far off Spartan warrior, carving his way through the hordes. The sheer quantity of blue gore that smothered him made him look almost inhuman.

Marlow must have blacked out from the pain because the next moment Dan was standing right over her, slapping her cheeks.

"Wake up!" screamed Dan.

Marlow looked around in surprise. All the Infiltrators had been slain, their icy innards rapidly crystallising and evaporating. The sky was a tornado of purple nebula that shot down to the still twitching body of the Darkmare. The creature was absorbing it all, its corpse swelling with ghostly purple light. The ground shook, increasing the collapse of the surrounding arena.

"The world is caving in!" Dan shouted above the chaos. "I don't think we should be here!"

Dan helped Marlow to her feet. She could barely stand. The kid was right - the nightmare realm was contracting into its creator. Beyond the shaking walls, the fracture into their own world was rapidly diminishing. Marlow didn't know what would happen if they were trapped inside, but every instinct told her it would be bad.

She stumbled again, leaning on Dan's shoulder for support. It gave her chance to study her unlikely saviour who was still clad in Infiltrator ichor.

"What happened to you?" Marlow wheezed. "Are you real?"

"I am, but this is still *my* dream. Well, together with my grandpa. So I'm the hero." Marlow couldn't argue with that. The sheer number of dissolving limbs around them and the fact monsters were running for cover from the kid were testament to his fearsomeness. "I'm the Dream Warrior," Dan added in just the right tone of voice to make him sound like the voice-over guy of a movie trailer. "Now - move it!"

Together they ran through the crumbling arena, towards the arched entrance through which the Infiltrators had carried the numerous cocoons. The wall was already shaking violently enough for clumps of resin to rain down across the exit. Marlow suddenly stopped and looked back at the sea of cocoons filling the arena, each one a captive person.

"What about them?"

Dan scanned the pods and briefly wondered if Maven and the other bullies from school were in there. If only Jade Harrow could see him now; then again, she'd always ignored him. He felt relieved that he didn't care. "There's nothing we can do for them. If we stay here, we're gonna get killed!"

Marlow felt a twinge of guilt, but the kid was right, she had a duty to return Dan back to his family in one piece. She had done it before, she'd damn well do it again. She tried to ignore the fact Dan was actually rescuing her.

"Maybe the pods'll protect 'em," Marlow volunteered, partly to ease her own conscience.

They charged through the Coliseum's archway as cracks spread across it with the tinkling sound of breaking ice. They burst into the arena beyond, into the tangled streets of both worlds, just as an Infiltrator sprinted in front of them, attempting to get back *into* the arena. Dan raised his sword high and bellowed at the top of his lungs.

The monkey-creature screeched. It was a sound that Marlow had never heard before and suddenly realised it was a cry of alarm. Dan swung the sword, but the creature adroitly sidestepped – eager to put as much distance as it could between them. No sooner had it run under the archway when the entire wall quivered, then collapsed in fragments on top of it.

Marlow's head was still reeling, and she was thankful Dan was guiding her in the right direction.

The earth tremor steadily grew worse as they approached the dwindling portal. The clouds forming the walls between worlds crackled as lighting licked across the surface and occasionally strayed free to stab the landscape.

Marlow stumbled, dropping to her knees, cutting them open on the sharp shards of crumbling residue. There was no way she could make it. Dan was already several yards ahead before noticing she was down.

"Go without me!" shouted Marlow. She knew she was finished. Dan had a life outside the dream; what did she have? "RUN!"

She saw the indecision on the kid's face as he slowly turned away.

Then, to her surprise, Dan turned back – and he looked furious. He sprinted back to Marlow, hauling her back to her feet with a strength that could only come from his weird dream-hybrid.

"You coward! How dare you!" screamed Dan. "I will not explain to your kids that you couldn't be bothered running out of here! They care about you! I care about you – so stop being so damn selfish and MOVE IT!"

The words shocked Marlow so much she suddenly found new reserves of energy. She grit her teeth, ignored the pain that consumed her. She ran.

The portal was yards ahead and now nothing more than the size of a doorway. Marlow increased her pace, shoving Dan ahead. The gap was closing so rapidly she doubted any amount of positive thinking would get her through.

Dan vaulted through it like an Olympian.

Marlow didn't have his otherworldly energy, so closed her eyes and jumped headfirst. She expected to feel the portal cleave her in two – instead she landed heavily in soft snow. She rolled onto her back in time to see the portal close with a loud pop, slicing the soles from her boots, which just hadn't made it across the line. The seething bubble of dream-world energy imploded with a hurricane blast that didn't affect the real world, but vaporised any Innerspace residue left behind.

The atmospheric force made Marlow's ears pop. Then silence.

She slowly stood and looked around. The town centre was almost demolished, but the cause was nowhere to be seen. Not a scintilla of evidence remained. Groaning bodies were scattered in heaps where the nether realm used to exist. Marlow had guessed right, the cocooned townsfolk had been protected from the multi-dimensional implosion that vaporised their protective pods. Now they were slowly regaining consciousness with no recollection of what had happened. Most looked confused and embarrassed to find themselves lying on top of total strangers.

Dan was bent over, hands on his knees as he fought to catch his breath. His sword and shield had vanished the moment the dream imploded, as had any illusion of super-human prowess.

He smiled at Marlow, too exhausted to say a word. Marlow grinned and gave him a thumbs-up. But Dan wasn't looking, he was peering behind her. She turned to follow his gaze.

Three kids were staggering through the throng, looking just as dazed and frightened as everybody else.

"Maven," said Dan with a slight scowl. Then gave a brief nod to the blonde girl he was leaning on. "Jade."

Maven raised a shaking finger and spoke through dry, cracked lips. "I saw you..." He frowned, desperately trying to recall an intangible dream.

Dan shrugged nonchalantly. "I get around."

Maven's bullish self-confidence had vanished. He could barely get the words out. "They... came. T-trapped us..."

"D-did he save you?" said Jade, unable to keep the awe from her voice.

Dan looked bashfully away.

"Kid," said Marlow, catching the girl's attention. "Dan just saved the world."

Dan soaked in their awe and admiration. Then they all swapped a puzzled look as they looked around.

"What happened?" Jade asked.

Marlow burst into laughter. Dan looked at her with wide eyes.

"Well that didn't last long. Welcome to the fortune and glory of being a Nightmare Hunter, kid."

. . .

DAN'S second reunion with his mother was just as emotional as the first. Unlike those who crossed into the other realm, her memories were intact. This time she was a lot more civil to Marlow, although she still was unsure what to make of her. In their smashed home, she recalled how she had made it to the ring road with Boris unconscious on the back seat, before the portal had contracted. The blast of displaced air had forced the car into a snow bank. Boris had woken up, rubbing the lump on his head and looking very confused.

He had been the last anchor the Darkmare had to the real world. Even in its final moments it clung to him to keep the portal open, but the further Boris was taken the weaker the bond became.

"So, I won't be having those nightmares anymore?" said Dan with a massive yawn. While he had been walking between both worlds, his narcolepsy hadn't affected him. Now it was all over, he was fighting to stay awake.

"That's right, kid. The Darkmare's not around to use you no more."

Dan nodded thoughtfully as he raised a cup of coffee to his lips. He stopped, then placed it down. "Then I suppose I don't need this." He shifted uncomfortably in his seat. "And I supposed I won't see you again." Dan had tried to keep his voice level, but a slight tremor gave him away.

Marlow and Bryony swapped looks.

"I think Miss... Marlow will be welcome here anytime. She may still have to keep an eye on you." She threw a glance at her father. "The both of you."

Dan didn't respond. He was fast asleep.

MARLOW PULLED up at the end of the street. This side of town had suffered the least from the Infiltrator's invasion. Most windows were boarded up, but people had banded together and covered the repairs with festive decorations as the town and authorities tried to come to grips with what had happened. The official excuse had been a gas explosion that had unleashed noxious vapours that caused memory loss and the occasional hallucination. Desperate for some excuse and a return to normality, the public hadn't questioned it. Now snow fell, making everything brighter and softer, eradicating even Marlow's terrors from the previous night.

She had spent hours in a trashed emergency ward to get her broken arm set and scars sewn. She'd just have to live with the ribs until they healed. The nurses had told her how lucky she was surviving the gas explosion. Many people were still missing.

Marlow returned to her apartment to shower and sleep a thankfully dreamless slumber. The water had turned black as she scrubbed her skin until it was red. She stared in the mirror as she painfully pulled a comb through her clean hair. Despite the recent hardships, she looked years younger. She was almost a stranger to her own eyes.

Then she took the most terrifying decision of her life. Facing the Darkmare had not been as frightening as choosing to visit her family.

She knocked on the door with a trembling hand. Then considered running before it opened. But she was too late. The door slowly opened, the faces of Jamie and Molly peered out from around the jamb. For a second they saw the face of a stranger.

Then they both broke into smiles.

"Mummy!" exclaimed Molly, running forward and hugging her tightly.

Marlow lost herself in the moment, then pulled a small wrapped package from her pocket and handed it to Jamie. For a second her son hesitated, unaccustomed to gifts from her, but then a smile creased the boy's face and he took it.

"Happy birthday, son. I didn't forget."

Marlow was guided inside, into a whole new life.

ALSO BY ANDY BRIGGS

SOME THINGS ARE BEST LEFT UNDISTURBED...

An **earthquake** strikes Los Angeles and brings with it a wake of
bizarre murders. Seismologist Michael Trent and LAPD detective
Alana Williams are brought together to investigate – but nothing
prepares them for what they uncover...

Something is emerging from beneath the earth – leaving behind
destruction and carnage.

Martial law is declared as the military battle the unknown threat.
Trent and Alana find themselves trapped between a hard line general
and invaders ready to trigger a **disaster** that will not only take out
California – but the rest of the world...

Printed in Great Britain
by Amazon